Better Than Perfect

Valerie Storey

Dava Books : Albuquerque

Better Than Perfect

Library of Congress Control Number: 2008909284

Young Adult fiction, published by Dava Books, Albuquerque, New Mexico.

Second Printing, 2016

ISBN 978-0-9643289-2-1

.... No; it's not
a world at all, but Pluto's
iron-black star; the quiet
planet furthest from the sun.

James K. Baxter, from "Thoughts of a
Remuera Housewife"

Chapter One

The last time I saw my mother, I was standing on the upper deck of the gull-white passenger liner, *Astor II*, while she, my only parent, remained below and infinitely apart from me on the crowded Southampton dock.

It was a warm English summer day, but I was wearing a woolen school blazer and thick socks because I was going into a New Zealand winter. No matter that my arrival was scheduled for six weeks away, I was dressed appropriately for my future and thereby signified a duty fulfilled and over. I was fourteen years old and too young in my mother's estimation to protest anything, least of all the absurdity of my clothing.

I remember clutching the end of a pink paper streamer. My mother, so different from me in her tall, blonde elegance, held the other end too casually for my liking, as though she were forced to play some foolish party game that demanded she be a good sport all the same. But then, she was with Lily Parker, and Lily hated sentiment. She hated it almost as much as she hated me. When the streamer suddenly snapped, bringing my mother's attention at last to what she held in her long hand, I fancied I saw an expression of relief cross her face. Her disgrace was finally leaving.

Embarrassed by her tactless ways, I looked down the side of the ship in an attempt to disguise my own troubled emotions. The hull was streaked with a salty rust not unlike the miraculous tears of a tin Madonna I had once read about in the Sunday supplements. The comparison disturbed me and with the vague feeling that my mother was something of a tin Madonna herself, I dropped my half of the streamer into the dirty foam beside the ship and turned away.

Nanny Braun, whom I had tried without success to conjure into nothingness, stood blocking my path. "Well, Elizabeth," she said before taking a deep breath. "This is it!"

I stared into her wrinkled, falsely smiling face, at the same time noting her too-tight summer dress and the ridges of the cheap corsetry beneath. Yes, this is it, I thought, keeping silent. The words thudded in my ears.

When Nanny Braun realized I was not going to reply, she amused herself instead by waving to the crowds below and humming, off key, to the strains of a brass band playing in the distance. Nanny Braun was a very raw and recent addition to my life; I had just met her that morning. She had been hired through an advertisement placed by Lily Parker in a newsagent's window. The advertisement promised a free passage to the South Pacific in return for looking after me.

Nanny Braun's arrival had been preceded by her five pigskin suitcases and a large photo album of the boys she was on her way to care for in Sydney. When she made her own overblown appearance, she hid her shock well, better than most people. Stoically, she ignored the squalor of our existence and in what seemed a matter of minutes she had packed my case, helped my mother into a blue silk dress, made Lily Parker a cup of tea and then eased us all into the taxi no one else had thought to order. She even remembered to ask, albeit with a good deal of innuendo, if I wanted to use the toilet, which I refused on principle. Lily Parker called her a gem several times before we reached the train station.

I didn't want a gem any more than I wanted to leave the messy flat in Kensington. I wanted to be with my mother the way she was years ago, before Lily Parker took over our lives and decided I was a nuisance. It was Lily's idea my mother send me "home," back to the family in New Zealand. "It's better all round," she insisted, though I was sure she meant better all round for Lily Parker.

Lily Parker frightened me and in many ways I was glad to escape her. She always reminded me of blood; her hair and freckles had the same sanguinary harshness I associated with aging vampires. As I stood on the slanting deck in the sun, feeling the prickle of damp wool at my neck and cheek, I shivered, but whether this was due to the past or to the future, I could not tell.

My fears were not made any easier when Nanny Braun finally said it was time to go to our cabin. "Your mother would want you to rest now," she said.

Silently, I surveyed this great hill of a woman before me

and thought what my mother wanted no longer applied. Disconcerted, Nanny Braun added, "You know, Elizabeth, you will have to speak sooner or later. Our quarters will be cramped and the time will pass slowly." It was not an attractive picture. I continued to stare and somewhat nervously, Nanny Braun held out her hand, indicating I was to take it in my own. Several years with Lily Parker had at least taught me the value of obedience, and I did as I was told.

Our cabin door was propped open with baskets of fruit and telegrams sent to Nanny Braun. Immediately upon entering what were indeed cramped quarters, Nanny Braun shut the door, then burst out of her dress in a series of small explosions.

"That's better," she moaned, fanning her face as she crumpled onto the narrow berth. She closed her eyes and sighed with drama as she succumbed to her first waves of seasickness, an amazing act, as we had not yet left port. I decided to leave her to her fate and took off my shoes and the blazer before climbing a short ladder to the bunk above her. There I stretched out full length and pretended I was having an adventure. It didn't work. All I could feel was a miserable sense of being punished, but what I had done eluded me. Glancing over the side of the bunk, I could just see the hand-painted lettering on the side of my case: *Elizabeth Haddon.* "Haddon" was underlined twice.

Perhaps my crime hid somewhere in that name, Haddon. I had been given my mother's maiden name at birth because she was not married at the time. And although I did not particularly mind or give the matter much thought, I know my mother did.

"Are you sleeping, Elizabeth?" came the weak voice of Nanny Braun. This time I felt like answering her, if only to voice my complaints.

"No," I said. "It smells funny up here."

"It's the oil. I expect we shall have to get used to it." Again she groaned and added, "Nanny doesn't feel her best now, so try and be a treasure and go to sleep." Another groan surged through the room, but this one came from the depths of *Astor II* as the ship pulled away from her moorings and struck out to sea. Our journey had officially begun.

For the next two weeks Nanny Braun did not feel her best, and then she promptly felt worse for the last four. We lived confined to the airless cabin, the telegrams collecting dust and the fruit slowly rotting until the steward eventually carried it away. The ship's doctor visited every afternoon, bringing pills Nanny Braun swallowed without effect. Five times a day meals suitable to our invalid status were left mostly untasted. Nanny Braun and I were both too ill for food, though for quite different reasons. Hers was an aversion to the sea, while mine was harder to place, being lodged in the cold anger of rejection.

Accepting despondency as a way of life, I hardly ever left the boundaries of my upper bunk. I lived in a sort of twilight sleep, punctuated by the magazines the steward delivered and nourished on the occasional cup of bouillon, that and my plots for revenge on Lily Parker.

Lying on my back, my nose inches from the green ceiling, I tried to place the exact date of Lily's arrival, but it was impossible. She had simply appeared, cluttered and malevolent, like the witch in a fairy tale. Suddenly the flat was filled with her thirteen hairbrushes, each one sprouting her crisp red hair, while rings grew like mold on the chair arms where she had left her endless cups of unfinished tea.

My mother saw none of this. To her, Lily Parker was the firm voice of reason in a self-created universe of confusion. Letting Lily Parker stay and make the decisions was easy, easier than telling her to go away, and my mother, who claimed to have a difficult life, required ease above all other material considerations. To her, Lily Parker was a power to be revered, and because of that power, I knew my vengeful schemes would bear no fruit.

I was able to dismiss Lily Parker one morning when Nanny Braun perked up before the steward brought our cold toast. Despite her warning that the two of us would have to depend upon one another for conversation, Nanny Braun had barely spoken the entire voyage unless it was to remind me of her great suffering. But today she could not hide her excitement. "We are here, Elizabeth," she said with strong emphasis on the "here." "Today you will begin your new life and we shall be finished with this dreadful ship. Never again, oh, never again…." For the first time since leaving home I felt a twinge of guilt, which I placed directly at the feet of Lily Parker.

Nanny Braun then proceeded to dress us for our disembarkment. Our clothes hung on us. Nanny Braun's winter jersey wool was nowhere near as tight as the first dress I had seen her in, and I had shrunk by several inches. The uncomfortable blazer felt enormous after the weeks I had spent dressed in my underwear.

"Whatever will your poor auntie say?" Nanny Braun wondered aloud in a flare-up of conscience as she perhaps realized she had not looked after me according to her contract. Yet so far, no one else ever had, and I thought it a bit late to start changing things now.

Leaving the ship was a complicated, boring affair of tips and tags and passports, but at last Nanny Braun was able to lead me with an exaggerated air of triumph down the blue and white gangway, into the freezing rain.

I had never felt so mean a cold. Nothing in London, famous for bad weather, had prepared me for it. Instinctively, I shrank back from its icy touch, a reaction Nanny Braun interpreted as shyness.

"Don't hold back, lovey," she said. "I'm sure your auntie's a fine woman. Do try and show her a more cheerful face than the one I've seen these last sad weeks."

Broadly smiling in the manner I was to imitate, Nanny Braun continued to use me as her shield against the weather as she propelled me toward land and my first encounter with my aunt.

Chapter Two

Oblivious to everything but her own sense of ceremony, Auntie Faye stood rigid beneath a black umbrella. Beside her was a slightly wet but otherwise distinguished looking man I knew to be Uncle Niall. Unlike Nanny Braun, neither of them was smiling.

I recognized Auntie Faye from photographs my mother used to have on the walls before Lily Parker took a dislike to them. Faye was my mother's eldest sister and she hadn't smiled in the photographs either. Single-handedly, she had raised the younger Haddon children when their father disappeared sometime after the Second World War and their mother gave up living for Lent, dying the subsequent Easter. My mother had been her chief disappointment, and Auntie Faye did not strike me as one to forget.

Nanny Braun gave me one last spirited shove, bringing me nearly face to face with my aunt's rubber-booted feet. "Mrs. St. James?" she asked as I picked myself up.

Auntie Faye shook Nanny Braun's fingertips. "Yes," she said. "And this is my husband, Dr. St. James, Niall."

Peering down at me, she added, "And this must be?"

She paused. "Little Elizabeth."

I ducked my head in reply and let myself be pecked on the cheek, grateful for the umbrella's shelter.

"Hello, dear," Uncle Niall said, taking over from his less gracious wife. "I suppose you want to get home and dry as soon as possible, eh? Your cousin Ravenna has been preparing your room for days."

Auntie Faye tightened her grip on the umbrella. "Niall," she said. "Why don't you and Nanny Braun go collect the luggage while I take Elizabeth to the car? The child doesn't look at all well." Giving Nanny Braun a disparaging glance, she turned on her heel and whisked me through the rain toward the visitors' car park.

"I expect you had a pleasant sailing?" Auntie Faye asked as soon as we were seated in the back of a roomy, new smelling car.

"We spent most of the time in bed," I said, chafing my ungloved hands.

"Seasick?"

"Nanny Braun was."

Auntie Faye pulled her fur collar closer and brushed the rain from my blazer. "This doesn't feel very warm," she said, lifting my lapel. "But not to worry. I believe Ravenna has a coat you can wear." She huddled further into her own coat and said, "Ravenna is looking forward to meeting you. Though you must remember, she is much older than you— as good as eighteen—and she has a very full schedule of activities. Ballet, elocution, hospital volunteer work; it's not the same world as when your mother and I were girls and there was time to stand still." Auntie Faye studied me thoughtfully. "Does your mother speak much of the past? Of our sister, Pat, and our brother, Morgan?"

As my mother had ceased to speak of anyone the day the photographs had been put away, I thought it best to lie: "All the time," I said. From the satisfied way she pursed her lips, it seemed the answer my aunt wanted.

"They are all at home, waiting for you," she said after a minute, turning to rub steam from the window. She looked through the hole she had made. "Ah, here are your bags."

"Most of those belong to…" I started to say, but Nanny Braun was wriggling across the front seat.

"My goodness, but it's cold," she said, tidying her hair in the rear vision mirror. "I hope it's not like this in Australia. My poor chest won't be able to stand another wet winter."

"Sydney is much colder than Auckland this time of year," Auntie Faye said when Nanny Braun sneezed. "How was your crossing?"

Nanny Braun took a crumpled tissue from her sleeve. "Dreadful. Of course, I'm not one to complain," she was quick to add, suddenly remembering who had bought her ticket. Leaning back and lowering her voice, she said, "Tummy troubles, you understand. Though I'm back to my old self already."

"You can lie down at the house if you like," Auntie Faye suggested. "Finding yourself thrust into the middle of a family reunion must seem a terrible bore. And you'll be wanting your energy for your trip to Australia."

Before Nanny Braun could say she loved family reunions, Uncle Niall took his place in the driver's seat. "Oh, thank you so much, Doctor," she said instead, turning to him. "I don't know how I'd have managed without you."

"Quite," Uncle Niall replied decisively, switching on the ignition.

The drive to Auntie Faye's house was made long by the heavy rain and constant chatter of Nanny Braun. For a woman who had not left her bed in weeks, she claimed to possess an uncanny acquaintance with the ship's social life. "The steward was an absolute sweetie," she said. "Tea and gossip every morning; isn't that right, lovey? Oh, the things we missed would make you weep. Racing and bridge, cocktail parties. But it couldn't be helped, could it?"

I sat by the door and let her talk wash over me like the rain. From this vantage point all I could see was the lead-black sky and acres of wet grassland. Yet Auntie Faye kept stipulating we were not in the country.

"You're quite mistaken," she said to Nanny Braun. "We are very urban. It's just that we have so much space and we don't build on top of one another like you do in the rest of the world." She made the rest of the world sound untouchably sordid.

We drove through more of the same ominous landscape until we came at last to a definite town and shopping area. Three more turns and finally Uncle Niall drove the car up a steep drive belonging to a house perched on a cliff edge.

"Home," Auntie Faye announced with pride. "I must say, however, it will be heaven to have things back to normal." She helped me out of the car and frowned toward the shrieks of adolescent laughter coming from the house.

A stiff wind off the ocean whipped my bare legs and blew the laughter away, at the same time shaking and bending the well-groomed shrubs and bushes that grew in a virtual maze of border hedges.

"Hydrangeas," Auntie Faye explained to Nanny Braun's admiration. "They thrive in this climate."

"I'm glad something does," Nanny Braun said. The fading clusters of blue, mauve, and ash-pink had an air of outdated royalty to them, like old ladies' hats, and I almost thought Nanny Braun was tempted to try one on. But Uncle Niall was shouting at her.

"I'll come back for the bags," he yelled over the wind. "Unless there's anything you want from them now."

"I don't want to impose," Nanny Braun yelled back.

Uncle Niall didn't wait to insist, and taking Nanny Braun by the arm, he led the way to the front door. Auntie Faye and I were close behind, but in seconds we had switched places, leaving Uncle Niall and Nanny Braun in the mud.

"We're home," Auntie Faye called out, pushing open the green and yellow storm door. She pulled me after her and immediately the sound of young people at play stopped as the passageway echoed with our footsteps. "We're home," Auntie Faye repeated, louder. Briskly, she marched me into the living room.

Gathered before me, caught like so many children playing statues was my long lost family, and for a moment, no one knew what to make of me.

Auntie Faye let her coat fall open as she hurried forward to marshal my way. "This is Elizabeth," she said, urging me to take center stage. "I'm sure we will all be friends, won't we?" Floundering in the unbroken silence, Auntie Faye glanced around the room for support. "Ravenna," she said to her daughter with relief. "Do come and say hello."

Slender, submissive, wanting to please, Ravenna left her window seat and came to me. "Hello, Elizabeth," she said, mixing flippancy with affection. She lifted her hair away from her face and because her mother wanted her to, she grazed my cheek with her own. Her skin was cold, as though she had been pressing hard against the window pane, but I did not stop to wonder, for there, imprinted in her perfect face, was my mother.

Not a single feature of my cousin could claim its own identity, all had belonged to my mother first: gray eyes sparked with silver, an upturned mouth that gave nothing away, a hint of tiny pale freckles on her straight, lean nose. Ravenna was very fine and I knew she was the child my mother should have had.

Her odd, half-kiss that bordered on insolence was the signal for the others to fall on me like the waves crashing outside the house.

The first to exclaim and wrap me in an overabundance of maternal warmth was Auntie Pat, my mother's middle sister. She held onto my hands, fighting back tears my mother would have died rather than show. "I never thought we would see you," she said, searching my face. "Your mother was so stubborn; she never wanted to share anything." She hugged me again while her American husband, Uncle Brian, grinned and squeezed my shoulder. Nearby, their two daughters, introduced as Wendy, fifteen, and Clare, ten, flushed and studied the floor.

"Don't smother the child," Auntie Faye said, looking on in disapproval. "It isn't healthy for either of you." Auntie Pat ignored her and continued her hungry inspection of me. Narrowing her eyes, Auntie Faye decided to get even by treating Nanny Braun like the new parlor maid. "Come and help me make the tea, Nanny," she said imperiously.

"Come and meet Uncle Morgan and Auntie Sheena," Auntie Pat said to me in a very different tone.

Morgan was my mother's only brother and the youngest of the Haddon clan. He and his wife sat on Auntie Faye's delicate, reproduction chairs with an expression just short of panic in their eyes, implying their visit was a rare one. When our first, fumbled introductions were over, Auntie Sheena thought it fit to explain themselves.

"We live on a farm just outside of Hamilton," she said as if apologizing. "We don't get up to the city much, but the next time we do, perhaps you would like to come back with us? Rory and Andrew would love the company." At the mention of their names, the two boys in the corner shuffled and spilled a deck of cards, their ears flaming.

Back in the room, carrying a loaded tray, Auntie Faye bustled over to us. "Now, Sheena," she said, revealing she had been listening because it was, after all, her own house, "Elizabeth won't have time to go down to Hamilton. Why, she's just arrived! We have to get her into school and making friends. And I'm not exactly sure a farm is the right place to do that, all respects to Rory and Andrew. But they're boys. And they're at that…age."

"Nanny?" Auntie Faye held out a rose-patterned cup.

Carefully taking it in both hands, Nanny Braun said, "I must tell you what a lovely house you have here. I'm certain dear Elizabeth will be happy; the place is so bright and cheerful. Not like the flat in London." A sudden downpour pounded the tile roof, drowning out her last words.

"What's that you say?" Auntie Faye asked, raising her own voice.

"Your house. Not—like—London."

I cringed, sensing my cousins' suppressed giggles as I resented a stranger's condemnation of my mother's household. Auntie Faye looked at me as though perhaps something had been said that should not have been, but she nodded anyway and asked if anyone wanted lemon.

I sat on the footstool beside Auntie Sheena, knowing that both of us were outsiders, and drank my milky tea. At least it was hot. And despite my dislike of Nanny Braun and her opinions, I had to admit she had a point about the house. It was definitely brighter than my mother's flat. The furniture was covered in good fabric and all the lamps were kept on, regardless of expense. I could just see Lily Parker righteously itching to turn each one off. "What a waste," she would have said, preferring the dark.

Auntie Faye tapped her cup with a spoon. "Ravenna," she said when she had everyone's attention. "I think you children have finished your tea. It's time you showed Elizabeth around."

"It's raining," Ravenna observed without moving.

"Honestly, dear. I didn't intend for you to go outdoors. I meant, show Elizabeth her room. Then perhaps you can all find a game to play."

At the mention of a game, Ravenna appeared offended, but she replaced her cup on the tray all the same. "This way if you're coming," she said to me, affecting a profound adult weariness.

I stood up to follow her to the door along with Wendy and Clare, but Ravenna abruptly turned back to her mother. "Should Rory and Andrew come with us?" she asked, barely hiding her disdain.

Auntie Faye was taken off guard. "Of course not. Not to Elizabeth's room." In a voice unused to dealing with her nephews, she said, "You boys go wait in the playroom while the girls are busy. They won't be long."

Rory and Andrew leapt at the chance to escape, and once again, Ravenna was in charge.

As she led the way to the hall, she indicated back to the two girls tagging behind us. "These brats are Wendy and Clare," she said, "in case you've forgotten. Wendy is the one who can't do anything with her hair and Clare's the baby. They both belong to Auntie Pat. You remember, she cries a lot."

"I'm not a baby," Clare said without any real conviction.

"Don't argue," ordered Ravenna. "Even Elizabeth is older than you." I took this to mean I had been admitted into the family hierarchy, but as to precisely where, Ravenna did not elaborate.

While we made our slow rambling way through the house, I sneaked a look back at my other two cousins to see if they also shared my mother's beauty. But instead, I saw faces as plain and ordinary as my own. As Ravenna had said, Wendy's hair was a frizzy brown mat, and Clare was so small and pale she seemed in danger of vanishing altogether. Yes, we were alike, united in a dull and persistent familial blandness to which Ravenna and my mother were the glorious exceptions.

My room was part of an addition built at an angle to the sea. Ravenna stood aside to let me enter first. "I've done it up specially," she said. "From a magazine."

I didn't know what to say. I could tell it was a nice room, the paint still smelled fresh, but it was somehow unnerving. "You shouldn't have gone to so much work," I said, thinking it was the sort of place where I would be expected to hang up my clothes and I would never be allowed to eat jam sandwiches in that smoothly made bed. It was also a great deal colder than the rest of the house.

Ravenna opened the drapes and fluffed a chair cushion.

"It wasn't anything," she said. "Just bits and pieces we had in the garage." She pointed to the wall. "I've put some old books on your shelves. You can read them if you like. I never do."

The shelves were beside a yellow pine dresser. Aware of the others watching me, I looked at the titles and realized I had read them all before. Yet I wanted to show my appreciation of Ravenna's efforts. "Thank you," I said, trying to mean it. "It's wonderful."

"Better than—London?"

I looked once more at the teal carpet and drapery. "It's pretty," I said lamely. "Very nice."

Ravenna sighed as if I were more stupid than she had first thought. "Not the room," she said. "What about your mother? What's your mother like?"

"My mother?" The question appalled me. "Why on earth would you want to know?"

The cousins erupted into nervous laughter. Trying to keep a straight face, Ravenna said, "Because she's…well, she's how we're not supposed to be! Or that's what Mummy always says." She lowered her voice and gave me a stern, disapproving look in imitation of her own mother. "'You don't want to grow up to be like Vida now, do you?'" she intoned. She laughed and resumed her own voice. "So what's she like? What makes her so terribly awful?"

I had no idea. "Terribly awful" was an epitaph I would have reserved for Lily Parker; my mother was merely lazy. "She doesn't do anything," I said, which was true enough.

Just getting her dressed was a chore.

Ravenna was disappointed. "Surely you can do better than that."

I looked into Ravenna's eyes and came out with the only other thing I could think of: "She looks like you."

Ravenna's face lit up. "Does she really?" She went to the wardrobe mirror and tested her profile in a variety of poses. "I wonder why Mummy never thought to tell me?" she asked, fascinated by her reflection.

From the other side of the room, Wendy and Clare were becoming bored. "We better find out what Rory and Andrew are up to," Wendy said, fidgeting with her hair. "Besides, your mother might come in here and ask what we're doing. You know she doesn't like closed doors."

Ravenna stood away from the mirror to get a different view of herself. "We don't have too much to do with Rory and Andrew," she said to me, tilting her chin. "They're terrible, too. Mummy says Auntie Sheena can't control Rory. And as far as Andrew is concerned, he's an idiot." She turned around, her color high. "He's always talking about dairy herds. Dairy herds," she repeated, sounding ill.

"Normally we don't have to see them," Wendy said, "but this is some kind of special occasion." I thought I detected a trace of resentment in her voice.

Before I could think any more of it, the four of us left the chill of my room and headed for the playroom that had nothing to play with and was in actuality a sort of study boasting a large television set. Rory and Andrew, deaf to

Ravenna's remarks, were doing nothing less vicious than sitting side-by-side on a boxy tweed couch, watching an ancient Western. As we joined them, Andrew spoke up as if on cue, "I'm getting a new calf. A heifer."

Ravenna and Wendy groaned, Clare swift to imitate. "Elizabeth doesn't want to hear about your horrid calf," Ravenna said.

We were spared further details when Auntie Faye came in search of us. "The boys have to be off now," she said turning down the television. "They need an early start if they want to get home in this weather. Let's say good-bye, girls."

We mumbled our farewells while Auntie Sheena appeared and repeated her earlier invitation to the farm.

"I'll think about it," Auntie Faye intervened, showing us all to the back door where Auntie Pat and Uncle Brian stood in pools of muddy water while they put on their raincoats.

"Going home?" Auntie Faye asked.

"Yes," said Auntie Pat. "I'm sure Elizabeth has had enough of her family to thoroughly confuse her for one day. I know I have." She laughed and tied a scarf around Clare's neck.

Auntie Faye opened the door and scanned the thunderous clouds. "You'll have to hurry," she said, lifting her face to the rain.

The other aunts, now dressed and ready for flight, hunched their shoulders, grabbed their children, and ran, side-stepping puddles and the wet shoulder-high walls of hydrangea. Not so cautious, their husbands turned back to wave at us.

"Regards to Niall," they shouted, startling me. I had almost forgotten Uncle Niall and to all appearances, so had Ravenna and Auntie Faye, though they continued to wave without showing any undue concern for the oversight.

When we could no longer see the tips of hats and umbrellas, Auntie Faye shut the door. "That's over," she said, eyeing her dirty floor. She started to reach for a mop and then stopped. Tuneless humming floated from the kitchen, halted by a muffled crash followed by a string of muttered threats.

"Oh, Nanny," Auntie Faye sang out with alarm, striding toward the noise. "There's no need to wash up. We have the girls for that."

Ravenna grinned. "Mummy used her best cups today. Just for you."

"That's right," said Auntie Faye as she pulled on a cardigan. "Which means, be careful!"

We arrived in the kitchen in time to stop the sugar bowl from sliding off the drain board. In spite of the noise, no damage had been done, but Auntie Faye was anxious Nanny Braun return to her regular duties. "Please, Nanny," she said. "Why don't you go into the lounge? My husband will make you a nice, tall drink." She took an apron from a peg by the stove and slipped it over her head.

Nanny Braun hesitated, soapsuds dripping off her hands. "I intend to do my share," she said stoutly.

"Then you can start by entertaining my husband." Victorious, Auntie Faye stood waiting.

Huffed by our intrusion, Nanny Braun dried her hands with some deliberation, glanced at her hair in the back of a saucepan lid, and then without another word went in search of Uncle Niall and the promised drink.

"Silly woman," Auntie Faye sniffed. She then focused her attention on an enormous leg of lamb, which she removed from the oven and placed on the bench with a satisfied thud.

"My mother doesn't cook," I said, watching her as Ravenna handed me cups to dry.

"You can't be serious," Auntie Faye said. "What in heaven's name did you eat?"

"Sandwiches," I said, trying to remember. "And sometimes we bought curries before the shops closed."

Auntie Faye strained meat juices into an empty marmalade jar. "It's a blessing you've come to me, Elizabeth," she said. "If your mother was too busy to even have the time to buy you a meal…."

"It wasn't that bad," I said, catching a secret smile from Ravenna.

"It was worse," Auntie Faye concluded. "Your mother should never have had a child in the first place," she added darkly. "She simply wasn't competent."

Ravenna gave the last cup a shake. "And she doesn't know a thing about clothes," she said, looking me over with distaste.

I wanted to fall through the floor. Nothing could have been farther from the truth. My mother loved clothes, but the gray skirt Lily Parker had deemed adequate for the colonies weighed and looked like concrete, and I knew it.

"Don't be rude," Auntie Faye said in a tone that implied Ravenna was right. "Tomorrow we can have a look through your wardrobe and find some things for Elizabeth to try on. It will be fun."

I hung my tea towel as neatly as I could on a wooden rack and asked myself what was fun about hand-me-downs; I'd read *Jane Eyre*. Then again, I wasn't stupid. Ravenna's clothes were the height of fashion. And if my mother couldn't be bothered to send me away decently kitted out, I could do without her. That would teach her to go around having children when she wasn't competent. Besides, I found myself liking this kitchen full of steam and electric light, warm while the storm blew outside. It occurred to me that neither Auntie Faye or Ravenna were the type to leave their brushes full of hair, and Auntie Faye would choose to be boiled alive before hot tea scalded and marked her furniture. Lily Parker, like yesterday's rubbish, wouldn't last a minute in this house.

"Ravenna," Auntie Faye said. "Go tell your father it's time to carve the roast."

A simple command, but so teeming with security and the chance to belong to a real family, that I listened with joy and wondered how I could stay forever.

Chapter Three

anny Braun stayed for two more days before Uncle Niall took her to the airport and sent her to Australia. She left with a pad of Auntie Faye's best recipes, promising to write and tell us if they were a success with the boys in Sydney.

For me she had the special request that I drop my mother a line as soon as possible and inform her of the delightful time we had spent on board ship together. As I had no intention of writing to my mother, this was dismissed as easily as I put aside Nanny Braun. However, erasing the actual physical memory of my mother was another story, especially when Ravenna not only looked like her, she never wanted to speak of anything else.

"Why do you always want to know?" I asked her the same afternoon Uncle Niall took Nanny Braun away. Auntie Faye was at a church meeting, something to do with new vestments for the vicar, and Ravenna and I were alone in the house.

It wasn't raining, but a storm still hovered in the air, making the sky dark and threatening. Ravenna had to sit under a lamp to sew new buttons on a dress she was giving me and the task absorbed all her frustrated attention.

"Your mother is exciting," she said at last, biting a thread. "Everything she does causes a sensation, or that's how it sounds coming from Mummy. I'd like to do something scandalous one day—oh, not anything really bad," she was anxious to assure us both, "but something just daring enough to be noticed. Make people sit up and stare and remember me." She gave the finished dress a gentle thump and tossed it to me.

"Here," she said. "You can wear this to church."

"What if I don't want to go to church?" I held the green velvet party dress to the light and thought wearing it to my equivalent of gloom and the grave was an absolute waste.

Ravenna closed her eyes, playing the martyr. "You mustn't say that sort of thing around here. Mummy thinks you're enough of a heathen as it is. She would keel over if she heard you now. Anyway," she said, "Mummy's determined to reform you and there's no use in struggling."

"I don't need reforming," I said boldly, feeling reckless with the adults away. "I need dance lessons and clothes and—things like yours," I finished, suddenly shy.

"Mummy reforms everyone," Ravenna said, a knowing look in her eye. "You'll see."

In the days that followed I waited to be reformed, but either Ravenna's predictions were premature or Auntie Faye was a master of deceit and I never noticed the subtle changes she affected in me.

Church was a prime example. The modern Anglican service we attended turned out to be a kind of sympathetic political meeting where instead of candidates vying for votes, everyone was already on God's side and therefore a winner.

Auntie Faye and Uncle Niall were popular with the congregation, due in part to their generous financial contributions, but also because of their social qualities. Uncle Niall's professional standing as a surgeon was respected and Auntie Faye was the one person who knew how to organize the jumble sales properly, keeping the used clothing separate from the fifteen-cent romances. And she was a stickler for dealing in only the tastiest baked goods. "Presentation is everything," she'd say, wrapping yet another date loaf in foil. Really, church wasn't so bad, and I thought my mother narrow-minded to be so strongly against it.

School was an entirely different matter. I started classes on the first Monday after the August school holidays, but as the year was next to over, Auntie Faye could see no reason for buying me a new uniform. Instead, I was equipped with the remnants of Ravenna's past.

"Nervous?" Ravenna asked me the morning I was adequately, if somewhat outlandishly, dressed.

"A little." In reality the prospect of stares and questions terrified me.

"You needn't be," Ravenna replied. "I don't expect you'll find anything very different from England. School's boring wherever you are.

"Here." She tossed me a snug black bathing suit we had

searched for a few days ago. "In case you're stuck in a swimming class."

I took one look at the limp knit suit and felt faint; somehow I would have to lose it.

Auntie Faye came into the kitchen as I was shoving the thing into a leather bag, a cast-off from Uncle Niall with a decidedly medical twist. She gave my blazer a critical look. "The sleeves seem a trifle off," she said, tugging them over my wrists. "But then everyone looks a fright in a school uniform." She handed me my lunch, then turned to Ravenna. "Don't forget you're on the afternoon shift at the hospital today, dear. Do you have a ride?"

"No, but I can get one."

"Good." Satisfied, Auntie Faye returned her attention to me. "The important thing to remember," she said, "is to mingle. Your mother never learned to mingle properly and she ended up with a very poor choice of friends. We don't want that for you, do we?"

"I can't imagine making any friends."

"Well, you won't with that attitude." Doing her best to look encouraging, Auntie Faye walked me to the door and front steps. "We'll see you back here at around four," she said. "Your little cousin Clare, you remember her, is to meet you at the school gates and walk home with you. When you get back we'll have a little party with Ravenna and Wendy. Won't that be nice?"

"Yes, Auntie." I turned to wave, but the door was already shut. I was on my own.

Cold air whistled up my sleeves, forcing me to walk faster than I wanted. Uneasily I told myself the situation was temporary; surely by the spring I wouldn't even need a jacket.

Reciting Auntie Faye's instructions that all would be well if I mingled, I found I had neither the talent nor the opportunity for the task, especially when I was compelled to search for my first class alone. Ten minutes after the bell, I handed a note from Auntie Faye to a teacher who ordered me to sit at the back of the room where I could not disturb his careful seating arrangements. He waited for me to choose a desk, silently counting, I was sure, each long second as I made my decision before he then plunged into a violent lecture on volcanoes. Not having studied volcanoes in England, I was at a disadvantage that became noticeable when I was discovered staring out the window.

"You girl!"

I looked up.

"Why aren't you writing?"

"Writing what?"

The teacher pointed with his chalk and smiled. "Writing what?" he repeated. The class cautiously echoed his laughter that stopped when he slammed his hands down on his desk and roared: "Volcanoes! What else?"

I tried to look attentive. I tried to take an interest. I desperately wanted to like volcanoes, but when the class was over, I still had a page almost empty of notes. As I was about to flee the room, he stopped me. "I'd like to see your exercise book," he ordered. I handed over my inkblots.

"You're Vida Haddon's girl?" he asked.

"She's in England," I said stupidly.

"She was also inept," he replied as if I had never spoken. "If you're to stay in my class you had better not let your heredity show through." He turned to wipe the board clean of lava and pumice and I ran.

I slowed down in order to find my next class and to also get my first real look at my fellow students. I noticed the girls' regulation uniform had changed since Ravenna had last worn it two years before. Although the differences were slight, a thin red stripe had been replaced with black, my uniform was dated enough to mark me as a charity pupil. The result was a math class worse than geography had been.

My social status continued to diminish and after a solitary lunch where I was shunned by students and teachers alike, I discovered my English teacher had also known, and never liked, my mother. She did, however, remember Ravenna more favorably. But as I had committed the offense of bringing the wrong textbook to class, even fond memories of Ravenna could not save me from a five-page essay to be written under her surveillance, and my first day of school ended both late and unmingled. Knowing Clare was supposed to be waiting for me, I also knew Auntie Faye would want a five-page explanation.

Although I was more than forty minutes late, Clare was still waiting for me, chewing on her hair. I had forgotten what she looked like, and when she came up to me I found it difficult to focus on her pale, receding features. If she hadn't had an odd, fish-like way of gasping every time the wind tried to knock her down, I would not have believed her there at all.

She made up for her hazy transparency though, with talk. "Where have you been? Auntie Faye will kill us!"

"I had to learn more about the school system," I told her. The answer seemed sufficient. Without her older sister, Clare was less timid than at our first meeting.

"You're lucky," she said as we climbed the hill home together. "Living with Ravenna must be heaven."

At nearly a head taller, I looked down at her white, white cheeks and her colorless lips. "It's not bad," I said warily. In secret I thought myself the luckiest person on earth, but it didn't do to boast.

Making one of her fish faces, Clare said, "Wendy thinks Ravenna's spoiled. She says Ravenna gets to do everything she wants. Everything."

I had my reservations about Wendy's judgment, but I let Clare's comment ride, leaving it to be eclipsed by the rest of her childish ramblings. Learning other snippets such as she would love to have a dog but Wendy was allergic, I finally led Clare into the house through the kitchen, something I believed would be Auntie Faye's preference.

"Are you sure Vida hasn't written?" It was Auntie Pat speaking, her voice coming high and shocked from the lounge. The mention of my mother's name made me stop and redden, as if it were somehow my fault she had not proved a better correspondent. I had not, after all, obeyed Nanny Braun.

"Of course I'm sure," Auntie Faye sternly replied. "How could I confuse a thing like that? There has been nothing, not so much as a postcard."

"I don't understand," said Auntie Pat. "It's very strange to me."

"Vida always has been strange," agreed Auntie Faye. "From leaving us three months prior to Elizabeth's birth, right down to sending the child back here because she was tired of being a mother. Not that she appears to have overworked herself in that department, but we don't even know how long Elizabeth is staying! It could be months, or years, or maybe she'll demand we pay some outrageous sum to fly her back next week! I know you'll think me harsh, Pat, but Vida is one of the most self-centered people I have ever known."

Clare looked up at me. "Are we going in or what?" she whispered, pulling my sleeve.

I jerked my arm away, unable to think straight, when a door squeaking told me Ravenna and Wendy were home.

"Why are you two lurking out here?" Ravenna demanded the minute she saw us. "What's wrong?"

"Everything," I replied.

Clare twisted around to face her. "Auntie Faye's complaining because Elizabeth's mother doesn't write letters," she said.

Ravenna gave her a withering glance. "Maybe she

doesn't like writing letters. I certainly don't." Dancing past us, Ravenna pushed open the not-quite-closed door to the lounge.

"Hello, Mummy. Hello, Auntie Pat." She turned to beckon us closer before fixing her full concentration on the laden tea table.

Auntie Faye had surpassed her usual skills: scones, jam tarts, chocolate and custard Napoleons topped with whipped cream greeted us. Wendy, Clare, and I clustered beside Ravenna, hardly knowing where to start.

"We've had ours," Auntie Faye said. "So help yourselves."

Eagerly, we loaded our plates, squabbling over the last Napoleon until Auntie Faye shooed us away. "You girls go on now," she said, not unkindly. "Auntie Pat and I need to talk."

I was sorry to leave, finding adult conversation more interesting than television, and I wanted to hear what else my mother had done wrong. Ravenna was apparently of the same mind, but she led us away when Auntie Faye sat motionless, refusing to open her mouth until we left.

We went to Ravenna's bedroom, a homier place than mine which still retained its magazine newness. Wendy and Clare gazed with undisguised envy at the collection of leotards, theater programs, and posters lining the walls.

"Have you got any new clothes?" Wendy asked Ravenna as Clare and I sat on the floor to eat.

Ravenna licked cream from the top of a scone before

answering. "No, not really," she said, her mouth full. "I had a good clean-out though, so I'll have to get some new things fairly soon."

Wendy opened the doors to the wardrobe. Scanning the still plentiful contents, she held out the skirt to a pale blue dress that shimmered as it caught the afternoon light. "I've never seen this before," she said accusingly.

"That's old. It doesn't fit Elizabeth yet, but Mummy wants me to hang on to it."

Wendy shot me a look of contempt I easily read as "hand-me-downs." She slammed the doors shut before taking herself to Ravenna's dressing table.

Ignoring her, Ravenna started a search of her own under the bed. After a moment she pulled out a cardboard box. "I wondered where these had got to," she said, lifting the lid and removing a red leather photo album.

Wendy sat down in front of Ravenna's mirror and unwound a lipstick. "Not photos," she said, stretching her mouth and testing the color against her lips. Rich plum turned to liver. "Not those photos," she repeated, angrily swiveling the lipstick back down into its case.

"Keep your hair on," Ravenna said, unperturbed by neither Wendy's hostility nor her failed makeup experiments. "Elizabeth has never seen these."

This wasn't entirely true. As I watched Ravenna flip through the heavy, old-fashioned black paper pages, I recognized the pictures of teenagers at the beach, and weddings where the young matrons looked on as a separate,

disgruntled group. They were all copies of the photos my
mother had once left out to remind us who we were. But
Ravenna was not interested in showing me these. Instead,
she continued flipping until she came to an oval-shaped
black and white enlargement obviously taken in a studio and
a long time ago.

"There," she said, laying it out on her bed. "Our mothers, when they were children."

Clare and I stood up and leaned over Ravenna's shoulder, fascinated. Our interest spiked Wendy's curiosity and
she condescended to join us for a second, bringing an eye
shadow palette with her.

"Can you guess who's who?" Ravenna asked.

I touched the tall, serious child wearing a shapeless dress
with a sailor collar. "Auntie Faye?" She must have been
about twelve years old, but already she had taken on the
cares of the world as she balanced a toddler on her skinny
hip.

Ravenna nodded. "That's your mother she's holding.
Funny, but it's the only shot I have of her. I think she must
have been the one with the camera for all the later pictures."

I carried on looking at the photo. Round, snub-nosed,
fighting to be free of her sister's embrace; my mother at two
was nothing like her present-day sophisticated self. I looked
closer. The small girl with tear-streaked cheeks had to be
Auntie Pat, and the sullen baby in a pom-pom hat was the
early version of Uncle Morgan. I thought the four little
Haddons stared out at us with as much discordance as they

suffered from today.

"They didn't have a very happy life," Ravenna said, as though some justification was needed for their long faces.

"Pooh," Wendy replied. "Their parents were still alive when this was taken. And anyway, it must have been fun being on their own after our grandparents died."

"That's a terrible thing to say." Disturbed, Ravenna smoothed the edges of the photo as if to soften Wendy's words.

Unconcerned, Wendy returned to the dressing table. "Don't you ever play like your mother was dead?" she asked.

Ravenna looked up in puzzlement. "Never," she said. "And I hope you don't either." She closed the photo album. "I swear, Wendy. Sometimes you say the strangest things."

Wendy laughed and Clare attempted to change the subject. "Mum's having a big party for Dad's business," she said.

"Are we invited?" Ravenna seemed glad to leave the topic of matricide.

"I think so. You usually are." Clare turned to me. "All the cooking is going to be done outside," she said. "Sort of like a *hangi*. Do you know what a hangi is?"

I shook my head. Winter was not my idea of picnic weather.

"A hangi," Wendy said for her sister, "is where you cook everything in a hole in the ground. Not what you'd call very exciting, but nothing in this place ever is. Anyway, Dad's built this sort of barbecue platform and claims it's cleaner."

"A hangi isn't dirty," Clare said quietly.

"Who asked you?" Wendy countered.

I wondered if we were in for another family reunion. "Will Rory and Andrew be there?" I asked.

Even Ravenna chuckled at that. "You must be joking," she said. "Inviting them would be a waste of time. They'd forget to come, or feed their invitations to the goats. Besides," she added more soberly, "they can't stand us."

"Why not?"

Ravenna sighed. "Because Mummy is forever telling them what to do. She hands out advice like Daddy dispenses prescriptions. Uncle Morgan gets angry and then they start to argue.

"When you arrived last week," she continued, "Uncle Morgan was on his good behavior. But now that's over, we won't be seeing any of them for a long time."

"Uncle Morgan used to run away from home when he was a boy," Wendy said idly, trying a blusher on her wrist.

"Because of the arguing?" I looked at Ravenna to see if I had touched on forbidden territory, but she said:

"That's part of the reason. The other is that he couldn't deal with his mother dying." She gave Wendy a pointed look. "Mummy says he took it personally, as though she went and left him on purpose."

"Which is ridiculous," Wendy said. "She had a disease. All her joints swelled up until she couldn't move. It might be hereditary," she said, giving Clare the evil eye.

Ravenna shoved the photo album away. "It is not.

Daddy said it wasn't and he should know."

"I wouldn't like that to happen to me," Clare said, almost to herself.

"It might." Wendy appeared to relish the terror spreading over her sister's face.

"Why must you be so hateful?" Ravenna intervened. "And stop fooling around with that perfume. I haven't got much left." Turning to Clare and me, she said:

"Don't listen to her. Daddy said none of us would become ill like our grandmother. It's impossible and I don't want to talk about it again." Abruptly, she lay down on the bed, her eyes wide open. "Nothing bad is going to happen to any of us. We are going to be happy for the rest of our lives. That's the way Mummy wants it and that's the way I want it. So there."

We were still for a moment, including Wendy who stopped and folded her hands, listening for more. Outside, the rain gently started up again, the first time in several days. As the drops splattered the windows, I looked at these cousins of mine and wondered if what Ravenna wanted could ever be true, at least for me. What if Auntie Faye was right and my mother suddenly called me home next week? Everything was so unsettled; I didn't have a clue where I belonged.

The rain continued and Ravenna closed her eyes as if she were drifting off to sleep. Watching her, I knew all I could do was to wait and to hope, and maybe, one day, I'd be as safe and as happy as she said I would be.

Chapter Four

That night I dreamed of Lily Parker; but she was called "Lily Fox" and she sang a sort of rhyme:

> *Lily Fox, Lily Fox*
> *Where do you hide?*
> *Under the earth*
> *Where all things die.*

In my dream I saw her seated before an electric fire, eating gingerbread she kept dunking in her tea. A trail of soggy crumbs littered the front of her ratty chenille dressing gown, and I could not take my eyes away. Then Ravenna somehow appeared in the room with us, her hair glowing scarlet from the fire. She asked me where my mother was and I replied, "Lily Fox ate her," and Ravenna screamed, "Who's a bloody little liar, then?" so loudly I woke up.

The rain had stopped, but my room was still cold. In the quiet night-filled house, I could hear the waves below softly breaking and I wondered if the dream Ravenna was right: Was I bloody little liar? Always so ready to deny my mother and the cool attraction she held for me, I had adapted too easily to my new life, too smoothly for my conscience to not be troubled. Yet the facts remained: my mother would not have me and I had nowhere else to go. Better to fit in where I could and have a life as close as possible to that of Ravenna's than live with the scorn of Lily Parker, I reasoned, rearranging my pillows. Far better than having nowhere else to go.

We received our invitation to Auntie Pat's party two weeks later. Auntie Faye showed it to Uncle Niall at breakfast.

"I assume we have to be there," he said without much interest as he continued to read a medical journal.

Ravenna tore the crusts off her toast and dipped them in jam. "I need a new dress," she reminded anyone who might be listening.

"Yes, to both of you," Auntie Faye replied. She studied the stiff white card she held as though deciphering a code. "I believe this has something to do with Brian's company," she said at last.

"That's so he can turn it into a tax write-off," Uncle Niall said, looking up. "Not that I blame him."

Auntie Faye paid no attention. "It appears all sorts of important people will be attending," she continued. "Listen to this, 'Guest of honor, Mr. Alan Trask.'"

Uncle Niall was faintly impressed. "Trask?"

I looked at Ravenna. "Who's Alan Trask?" I whispered. She shrugged and shook her head. Auntie Faye was smiling as she propped the invitation on the windowsill.

"That's right," she said. "Alan Trask. Of the supermarket chains," she added. "Old money. And I particularly want you, Ravenna, to make an impression on him."

Ravenna's eyes took on a look of horror. "Me? I don't have to meet him, do I?"

"Of course you do," Auntie Faye said. "You're young, fetching, graceful, and very well spoken. And if you play your cards right...."

Ravenna appeared stunned. She looked to her father for asylum, but he kept his gaze back on his medical journal, firmly out of this particular domestic development.

"What do I have to do?" she finally asked her mother.

Auntie Faye's smile grew wider. "Nothing very difficult, dear. Be friendly; uphold your father's name. You can do that, surely?"

"If you say so."

I felt like something was expected of me, so I volunteered, "What about me? What do I do?"

Auntie Faye laughed. "Just stay out of hot water, Elizabeth, and enjoy being fourteen and carefree. It doesn't last."

She returned to washing the dishes. "I wonder if Pat would like me to make some of those chicken *vol-au-vents* I made for the Hymnal Society luncheon last month," she said more or less to herself. "They did go down rather well. Or what about sausage rolls? Except they are getting to be old hat these days."

Uncle Niall spooned the last of his boiled egg. "Parties,"

he said. "Once you women start scheming with your menus and matchmaking, the whole country could fall apart and you'd never notice a thing except the state of your pastry shells."

"It's for a good cause," Auntie Faye said dryly. "Helping one's husband get ahead in life is not necessarily a frivolous pursuit." She looked toward both Ravenna and me. "You girls remember that," she added.

I wondered how she had jumped from telling me to enjoy being fourteen to helping a future spouse get ahead in life. Ravenna's response was to nervously butter more toast.

"Auntie Pat met Uncle Brian at a bus stop," she told me. "He was an American who came down to marry someone else but his fiancée ran off with this unemployed actor at the last minute so he married Auntie Pat instead. Isn't that romantic?"

"Don't gossip, Ravenna," Auntie Faye said, her voice suddenly testy as she cleared the table.

"It's not gossip! Auntie Pat tells that story all the time."

"Not like that, she doesn't. You make it sound like the script to a cheap film." Auntie Faye turned to Uncle Niall, her hands full of dishes. "Will you be home tonight?" she asked.

"I think so. I've got a surgery scheduled for the morning and I want an early night." He stretched and got to his feet, taking his magazine with him. "Well, girls, I'll see you later. Enjoy your circus."

Ravenna rose part way from the table to kiss her father's

cheek. "What circus?"

"Getting ready for this blasted party. Buying new clothes. All those useless things you females spend my money on."

"Oh, Daddy. Don't tease," Ravenna said, watching her father leave the room. When he was gone, she said, "It's true that I need a new dress."

"I know, I know," Auntie Faye said from beside the sink, scraping plates. After a moment she said, "I think Elizabeth can wear that green velvet you've fixed so nicely, Ravenna."

"She's worn it to church twice."

"And she's just at that age where she'll be outgrowing it in no time so it's a waste to buy something new." Auntie Faye looked back over her shoulder at me. "You do understand, don't you, Elizabeth? I'm not trying to be mean, just practical. When you're older it will make sense to buy new clothes, when all this growing business has settled down a bit."

I nodded, not overly concerned. I liked the green dress fine and I was more preoccupied with the morning's impending math test than new clothes.

In the days between receiving our formal invitation and attending Auntie Pat's party, Auntie Faye organized our lives with the efficiency of a drill sergeant. There were phone calls back and forth to Auntie Pat, shopping expeditions for Ravenna that had to be fitted between dance classes, and my first lessons in rolling out puff pastry.

The one sour note was a letter finally arriving from my

mother so late and ill-timed that it was first a subject for ridicule and then one of neglect. Two pages long and on the smallest airmail paper available, my mother had written to say she hoped I was settling in and that Lily Parker, as if any of us cared, was well. I thought it was the type of letter that should have had a postscript saying the cat had died in my absence, but we didn't have a cat. Lily Parker, like Wendy, was "allergic."

The party was scheduled for a Saturday, my day to clean the bathroom, leaving Ravenna free to lock herself away with her new dress. "Wait and see," was all she would tell me about it.

I thought it was fortunate for Auntie Pat the morning had brought no rain. Still, the sky was overcast and the air cut like ice, and I knew there was never any telling what could happen later. I shivered, clenching my teeth as I scrubbed tub and tiling with water so cold my hands swelled with the red pain of it. As soon as I could I bounded back to the kitchen where the oven had been working overtime all morning.

"You should get dressed now," Auntie Faye said as she glazed her final tray of sausage rolls. The bench beside her was crammed with foil-covered trays, the product of four-hours-straight baking. "I don't know what Ravenna's up to," she added. "I haven't seen her once. Would you mind checking on her and telling her to hurry, please?"

Reluctantly, I left the warmth of the kitchen and knocked on Ravenna's door. "It's me," I said, swinging on the doorknob as I peered inside.

Ravenna twirled around like a model. "Do you like it?" she asked, her eyes shining silver.

I stopped, horrified. There were no adequate words to describe how fresh and pretty and summery she looked in a crisp blue and white striped linen dress with a matching jacket or how worn and saggy my own dress would look next to her.

"It's great." I also saw she had done her hair in a new way, sweeping if off her face with a pair of blue enamel combs. That, and her new high heels made her look at least twenty. "Lovely," I mumbled, wishing something terrible would befall and let me stay home.

Auntie Faye crept up behind me, smelling of warm butter and flour. "Oh, very smart," she said in approval. "You won't be cold?"

Ravenna smoothed her hair. "I've got a tee-shirt on," she admitted, adjusting a comb.

Remembering I was still in a pair of badly fitting corduroy jeans, Auntie Faye said, "Don't stand there gaping, dear. Go and get ready. I promised Pat we would help serve."

I regarded her with stony detachment for a quiet second before dragging myself to my room. Once there, I pulled the green dress from the hanger and wondered what I had ever seen to like about it. What I had once thought sweet and Victorian now appeared just plain old. The velvet pile, I noticed, was crushed in the seat, and Ravenna had sewn two of the textured buttons crooked. It was a horrible dress and it was horrible of Ravenna to show me up like this.

I undressed in a hurry, purposefully leaving on my hole-ridden Saturday underwear in the angry hope we would have a car accident and the entire family would be shamed into ruin when I was wheeled into the emergency room less than well-groomed.

My scowl stayed in place as I went back to Auntie Faye and the kitchen, but she was too busy to notice I had even changed my clothes, let alone my mood.

"Here," she said. She thrust a stack of boxes at me. "Take these to the car. Your uncle is having a positive fit over the time and there's still my hair to fix!"

Ravenna came in at last to do her share, but she would only take one box and that very delicately, being frightened of getting grease on her skirt. "I'd hate to dirty it," she said, happily ignorant of the replies that rose to my lips.

The trip to Auntie Pat's was quick and without event. She also lived close to the sea and because of the way her house was placed behind a row of summer cottages, we were forced to park the car at a distance and carry our trays and boxes down a winding gravel drive.

"I think we must be early," Auntie Faye said, looking into the vacant windows of the cottages we walked past.

Uncle Niall grunted at the thought of any kind of time for the party, early or late, but he switched on a friendly, professional smile when Wendy and Clare called from the porch to greet us. Upon seeing them I felt a weight fly off; they were dressed just as badly as me.

"How charming," exclaimed Auntie Faye, taking in their identical pintucked red pinafores. A large polka-dot giraffe was appliquéd to the front of Clare's pocket from which sprung an olive hankie. Wendy was spared the giraffe but not the handkerchief. "Did your American grandmother send you those?" Auntie Faye asked.

"How did you know?" Clare sputtered, surprised. Wendy's face turned the exact shade of her dress.

"Well, they're very—novel," Auntie Faye said, pouncing on the aptness of the word with relief.

"Oh, Faye. Let me take those." Auntie Pat came out of the house toward us. "Doesn't Ravenna look grown up?" she said, smiling at her. "And that green is very becoming, Elizabeth. It never did suit Ravenna."

Unhappy with a compliment phrased as a reminder of my "poor relation" footing, I hung back a step or two, but Auntie Faye hurried me indoors with the rest of them.

Once inside, Ravenna and I were placed in the care of Wendy and Clare with the strict instructions to go away until we were called for.

Wendy's humiliation was hard for her to bear because it was the first thing she spoke of when we were alone. "It's our grandmother's fault," she complained. "She sends these awful things out and we have to wear them. And since she hasn't seen me for ten years, she thinks I'm still five years old." She glanced sideways at Ravenna's stylish outfit. "You look nice," she said as if the words burned her tongue.

Ravenna looked down at her new shoes. "Fat lot of

good it does when I get ordered off with the children."

"We get to help pass out the canapés," Clare said in consolation. "Isn't that neat?" But I could tell Ravenna was not impressed.

Wendy and Clare took us to a small glassed-in patio area at the side of the house. Potted ferns and white cast iron furniture gave the place a sunny, tropical feeling and it was easy to forget the bitter cold outside.

"I love this room," Ravenna said, standing close to a radiator. "I keep asking Mummy if we can do one like it ourselves, but she doesn't seem to listen." Ravenna rubbed her hands together over the heater and then went to sit on one of the chairs, careful to guard her skirt from creases. Her eyes moved without rest, and then stopped when she spotted an easel propped against the wall, a sheet draping the canvas it held.

"Is your mother starting to paint again?" she asked.

"No," Wendy replied. She crossed her arms to hide the unsightly handkerchief. "It's just her usual dabbling. She isn't an artist. Not like Rory." The three girls burst into private laughter, leaving me perplexed and out of the joke.

"Rory paints?" I asked. No one had ever mentioned either him or Auntie Pat for that matter, as being interested in art.

Ravenna checked her mascara with a tissue. "He thinks he does," she said. "He has some crazy idea he'll become an artist one day, painting pictures of sheep and chickens, no doubt." This time her laughter was ruthless.

"Stupid, isn't it?" Wendy said, trying to steady her own voice.

I hungered to be part of their laughter, but I didn't understand the joke. "Why is wanting to be an artist stupid? I think it sounds admirable."

"Oh, Elizabeth," Ravenna said, dropping her voice to sound like her mother. "Sometimes you can be so dense. How can a grown man make a living as a painter? I suppose he could teach, but it's not as though he could be very successful."

"My mother knew several men in London who were artists," I said. "None of them were teachers." They weren't very successful either I realized when I gave it some genuine thought.

For once Ravenna did not want to hear about my mother or her friends. Primly covering her knees with her skirt, she said, "This isn't London. People have to fit in."

"Fit into what?" Immediately I thought of narrow shoes and jelly molds.

Ravenna gave me a critical look. "Society, what else? Listen, when Rory says he wants to paint, it's just a way to grab attention—something to make trouble and get everyone worried." Having pronounced judgment, Ravenna looked around for challengers, but she was saved further argument when Auntie Faye leaned into the room.

"There you are," she said, sounding not a little frantic. "Do hurry up, Ravenna. Alan Trask has just arrived and absolutely no one is eating the sausage rolls!"

Auntie Faye herded us back into the large, high-ceilinged living room now filled with men in casual business attire and women wearing everything from jeans to striped caftans. Headed by Auntie Faye, they formed a circle around a tall, conventionally handsome young man Auntie Faye whispered to me was Alan Trask. I thought he looked boring and safely non-artistic, but Auntie Faye sharply pulled me away from my reverie. We weren't here to dawdle, she told me, not when ten trays of *hors d'oeuvres* awaited consumption.

After giving Ravenna a little shove in Alan's direction, she drew me, Wendy, and Clare into the kitchen and gave us each a tray to carry with explicit orders to empty it posthaste.

"Mingle," she commanded.

Wendy and Clare were obviously well-schooled in the art of enticing strangers to eat finger foods. Even their matching dresses suddenly seemed appropriately waitress-like and I wondered if that's why Auntie Pat had insisted they wear them.

I didn't share their expertise. Several steps behind, I kept offering tid-bits to guests with full plates. When my own offerings were routinely refused, I had no choice but to return to the kitchen and Auntie Faye.

As soon as she saw me, she stopped folding cocktail napkins into fluted triangles. "Your tray is full," she said.

"Wendy and Clare got to everyone before me."

"No excuses," she said, sending me right back out. "And remember to mingle."

I took my tray into the middle of the room and watched

Alan Trask ignore Ravenna as completely as everyone else
had waved away me and my pastries. We were both saved
further effort when Uncle Brian came in through the French
windows and gestured with a fork toward the barbecue pit
and a cloud of smoke. "Chow's up!" he announced.

The guests turned as one with Alan Trask as their designated leader, emptying the room of their loud chatter in
seconds. Ravenna, Wendy, and Clare stayed behind with me
in what had become "the children's group."

"What do I do with these?" I asked Ravenna, showing
her the tray.

"How should I know?" She stared out to the patio
where Auntie Pat's guests were lining up for steaks and
butterfly shrimp. "Throw them away."

I gave her a curious glance and nearly asked what I'd
done wrong now, but Wendy answered for her. "Alan Trask
didn't ask her to be his dinner partner."

Ravenna blushed to the roots of her hair. "Don't be ridiculous!"

Wendy smirked. "Aren't we the touchy one?"

Ravenna glared and suddenly tore off her jacket. "It's
this fabric. Nobody said it would be so scratchy. I had no
idea linen could feel this bad. And look, I've torn my
stocking. Not that anyone cares." She held out her leg to
display a ragged hole. She grimaced and in an instant
became one of us again.

"I have an idea," she said, turning to Wendy and Clare.
"Do you think there's a chance we could take some food and

go somewhere else?"

Wendy hesitated, but Clare was jumping up and down. "Yes, let's," she said. "Please, Wendy. Please say 'yes.'"

Wendy looked at Clare and me and then to Ravenna. "What about your dress? Your shoes?"

"I don't care about them. Lend me a pair of running shoes or something."

Later, without her high heels and wearing an old nylon parka of Auntie Pat's, Ravenna looked as absurd as the rest of us.

"Now where?" Wendy asked, her arms loaded with packages wrapped in newspaper.

Ravenna thought for a minute. "I know a place that's secret and where no one will bother us."

"What secret place?" Clare demanded, mystified. "I've lived here my whole life and I've never seen any place like that."

Ravenna didn't stop to answer and instead, led us outdoors and to a path on the far, lesser-used side of the cottages. The entrance was blocked by fallen branches and discarded milk crates we had to step over to reach a narrow trail paved with powdered seashells. Straightaway we were enveloped in a damp green world of moss and towering tree ferns, at once both sad and mysterious, causing a lump to stick in my throat for no explainable reason. The others must have felt it too, for we walked in silence until the path abruptly ended in a wooden staircase and the sea.

"Mum doesn't like us to go this way," Clare said, her

words punctuated by the harsh cries of the gulls overhead. "She thinks it's risky."

Ravenna looked past her. To the left was a pine grove atop a steep, grassy hill. "I want to go up there," she said. "But be careful. There isn't a path."

Again we followed her up through the thick grass, the wind blowing our hair into our eyes, making me stumble.

"Not much farther now," Ravenna panted. She took some of the wrapped food from Wendy.

I felt as though we would never stop climbing, but at last we reached the trees. There we paused to catch our breath before scrambling down to our destination, a deep ledge of rock jutting over a small waterfall and the deserted beach.

Heedless of her dress, Ravenna sat down first, leaning back against the protection of the hillside. "Come on," she said, holding out the food we had brought. "It's perfectly safe and the wind doesn't reach when you're sitting."

Hunger overcame fear and we joined her as we discovered there was plenty of room to rest and eat without tumbling over the sides. For a few moments we were content to meditate, chewing slowly and watching the choppy sea.

Ravenna wiped her hands on the front of her blue and white skirt, leaving streaks of mud, food, and grass stains. Her hair had come loose and even with the smudges of dirt on her face I thought she had never looked more beautiful. Auntie Faye would be furious, but I was glad Alan Trask hadn't asked her to be his partner. It was wonderful to have her alone, away from the adults. She gazed out to sea and said, "You could think this was the last place on earth."

"It is the last place on earth," Wendy quibbled.

"No, it isn't," Clare said. "The South Pole is."

Ravenna smiled. "It's *taniwha* country."

Clare covered her ears. "Stop it. I don't like those stories."

Ravenna's smile widened and I suddenly felt like an outsider again. "What are you talking about now?" I asked helplessly.

"A taniwha is a monster," Ravenna explained. "From Maori mythology. It's like a huge lizard, much bigger than a human. It comes and steals young girls and takes them to its underwater cave."

"Don't!" Clare squealed. "I hate the taniwha."

"Have you ever seen one?" Ravenna asked her.

"No."

"Then how do you know you hate it?"

Clare threw the remains of a lamb chop into the bushes. "I just do," she said. "He's bad. And ugly, too. Yuk. Fancy being stolen by a horrible old lizard."

Ravenna hugged her parka closer. "I always feel sorry for it."

Wendy laughed. "Why should you? It's a stupid story. How can you believe something like that?"

"Easily. When I was little I used to think the taniwha was real. Just like Clare."

"I don't think it's real!"

"You could have fooled me." Ravenna studied her cousin for a second, and then said, "I used to worry terribly that he would climb into my room. But then all of a sudden, I don't know why, I felt sorry for this poor, frightening monster that had to steal a bride because no one wanted him for himself. I thought that if I ever saw him, I'd try being nice to him. I'd tell him I wasn't afraid and then he might be nice and go away."

"What rot." Wendy laughed again and kicked a stone, sending it flying into a small avalanche down the hill.

Ravenna shot her a critical glance. "There must be something to it," she said. "People don't make up stories without a reason." She faced Clare again. "The taniwha could still come at any time, when we least expect him, and you have to know what you're going to say to him. You have to."

Clare was close to tears and I thought this monster talk had gone on long enough. The tide was starting to pull out and I could see the tops of what looked like oyster beds appearing through the water. I stared at their sharp, rough edges and thought of my mother and Lily Parker. "Do you think we could go down to the sand?" I asked, trying to get away from the image.

"There'll be sandflies," Wendy said.

Ravenna gave me a smile that told me what Wendy thought didn't matter. "I'm game," she said. "Anyone else?"

"Well, I'm not staying up here without you two," Clare

said. She all but danced to be leaving the place.

"Thanks a heap, Sis," Wendy said, rising to her feet and leading the slippery descent to the shore.

My legs were shaking by the time we reached the beach, but Ravenna was in high, fierce spirits; our final, downhill slide exciting and liberating her. Flinging her arms out to her sides, she shouted some wild war cry of her own making and tore off running down the length of the sand. Not to be left behind, we followed close, screaming along with her at the top of our lungs, racing each other and the tide until we could run no more.

"That—was—super!" Clare choked out, gasping and giggling as she hopped from foot to foot, the taniwha forgotten. "We should go up there again someday," she added, confident we would remain a group. When no one answered her, Clare's forehead crinkled and she fell silent.

Ravenna must have sensed some of her dismay. She reached out and drew Clare's hair back into a ponytail. Fastening it with a rubber band she pulled from a pocket in the parka, she said, "I don't think we'll be going back any time soon."

"Why not?"

Ravenna shrugged and I wondered if she was still thinking about the taniwha, but all she said was, "Mummy. Life." She looked down at her ruined dress. "Society."

I hurried to agree with her. "That's right. What if someone saw us just now? It's fine for you, Clare, to run around screaming, but Ravenna and I, and you too, Wendy, well, we have to be more careful of what people think. So we can, you know, fit in." I hoped I had got it right this time and I looked to Ravenna for approval.

But Ravenna didn't reply and instead, a heavy mood of desolation settled around our shoulders like wet strands of seaweed. Instinctively, I moved closer to her side, inwardly seeking what I believed to be a kind of strength, one born of poise and confidence and all that Ravenna symbolized for me. Yet she gave no sign that she had noticed my need for her, and I began to feel I was at the bottom of the world in more ways than one.

Chapter Five

S ummer and the telegram from my mother's solicitor
arrived together exactly three weeks before Christmas.
It was a warm, rainless afternoon calling for shorts
and bare feet, luxurious attire after the winter months.
Ravenna and I were finally freed of school, but only I was
allowed the indulgence of lying on the lounge floor with a
book; Ravenna still had to maintain her schedule of what
Auntie Faye referred to as "learning the social graces." I had
no idea where she was on her way to today: flower arrang-
ing; Cordon Bleu cookery; community service teas with the
elderly. She never seemed to stop.

I could hear Auntie Faye busy with someone at the front
door and when she closed it, Ravenna shouted, "Mummy,
do you have any idea where my tap shoes are?"

A lack of reply brought her into the room. She glanced
at my book, shrugged and turned when Auntie Faye entered.
"Mummy, where are my...?" Something in Auntie Faye's
eyes made her back uneasily to a chair. "What is it?" she
asked. "You look awful."

"Do I?" Auntie Faye sounded surprised. Automatically

she reached to smooth her hair, but her movements were rough and the pins holding her waves in place bounced soundlessly onto the carpet. For a moment she stared at them shining in the sunlight, her hair hanging disheveled over her cheek.

"Let them be," she said when Ravenna sprang forward. She went to the gold settee beneath the window, twisting a slip of yellow paper between her fingers.

Ravenna stood still, watching her mother's hands work and re-work the paper into a ball. "Is it bad news?" she asked in a small voice.

Auntie Faye drew several breaths before answering, and then, as though the very name meant bad news, she said, "It's Vida. Elizabeth's mother has been in an accident with that Lily Parker person. She is dead. They both are."

I heard, and did not hear. The afternoon sun poured down onto the velvet furniture, striking the dust motes with rainbow rivers of color I let myself melt into. I was flying on wings of color, far away....

"Oh, Elizabeth!" Ravenna's arms were around my neck, shocking me back into the present and dissolving the rainbow.

Instantly, I shook loose, breaking off her sympathy in order to have the strength to face my aunt. "How?" I asked.

Auntie Faye looked down at her fist and opened it, letting the crushed telegram quietly unfold like a yellow rose. "Your mother and that woman must have been on holiday. They were driving up to Scotland and the brakes gave way."

I pictured my mother and Lily Parker flayed on the pavement like the butchered rabbits sold in London's outdoor markets, and I shuddered, all the fight and summer's warmth gone out of me. Ravenna must have felt some sense of my defeat, for she suddenly left me to kneel by her mother's lap in fear.

"What will we do?" she asked, quivering like a small child.

I didn't wait to find out. The airless lounge was stifling and I turned and fled to the bathroom, a place I knew for certain had a locking door. I flung myself against it while I tried to understand.

My cramped surroundings stood out in sharp, mocking detail like puzzle pieces from a dream. The plastic flowers, the knitted skirts of the doll disguising a toilet roll, the bath sponge the color of dried apricots; all loomed before me with a surreal sense of disaster. My mother and her best friend were dead and I was soiled with death three weeks before Christmas. My presence in the house spoke an evil omen and my first thought was to wash the stench of it away. I stripped off my top and shorts and turned on the taps full blast.

The shower pummeled my scalp, keeping my mind at bay and my throat from gagging. I stood there like a dead thing myself until the water went cold and I could hear Ravenna screaming at me to come out as she shook the door on its hinges. Finally, I shut off the water and draped a towel smelling of artificial sun and lavender under my arms before opening the door.

"You've been crying," Ravenna said, sounding out of breath.

"I've been taking a shower. My face is wet from the shower." I rubbed my face dry with a corner of the towel. "See?"

"Well, you should be crying," she said, handing me a clean set of clothes.

"You're not."

"She wasn't my mother. I never knew her."

"Then that makes two of us," I said.

Ravenna looked hurt by my reply and I was immediately sorry. "I just feel like she's always been dead," I explained. She seemed to want more, and I added, "She wasn't like a real mother. Not like yours. She was…she was just different."

"Look, if you want to cry—"

"I don't want to cry."

Ravenna started to speak, then changed her mind and thrust her hands into her hair with frustration instead.

"I can't help the way I feel," I said.

"You should!" Ravenna cried bitterly. She gave a little sob of incomprehension and ran away down the hall, leaving me devastated. Nothing was making any sense and I was ashamed of my hard heart.

I closed the door and dressed slowly, wondering what Auntie Faye would do with me now there was no specific obligation to take me on as a worthwhile cause. Forsaken beyond measure, I left my shoes and went to my room to escape in sleep.

It was dark when Ravenna jarred me awake. "You've got to come out now," she said, slightly recovered from her earlier outburst. "Mummy said to leave you alone before, but now Auntie Pat is here and she's asking for you."

Still sleepy, I sat up, trying to remember what had happened. "Why is she here?"

Ravenna crossed the room to leave. "This is a family tragedy," she said, meaning it.

I pushed away the blankets and followed her back to the living room and Auntie Pat.

Auntie Pat was crying without restraint when we joined her in the other room. "You poor, poor child," she said when she saw me, her gestures loose and expansive, giving me the impression she was somehow dressed in her nightie rather than the cotton shirtwaist she kept severely belted.

"There, there, Pat." Auntie Faye pried her sister off me and took her to a straight-backed chair. "Try not to cry anymore."

With Uncle Brian looking on uncomfortably from the opposite side of the room, Auntie Pat continued to cry whether her sister liked it or not, and I could tell Auntie Faye's patience was coming to an end. I also noticed her hair had been pinned back in place against further accident and her makeup had undergone repairs. Auntie Faye had managed to take control of her emotions and she now expected the same from everyone else.

"This has been a terrible shock for everyone," she said, "but we have to carry on, for the future." I felt her hands guide me to the settee with Ravenna who moved over to make a space for me. I watched Uncle Niall bending over the cocktail cabinet before turning to hand the adults a silver-etched sherry glass each.

"To the deceased," he said, lifting his glass formally to the light before downing the contents.

Uncle Brian and Auntie Faye followed his Spartan example, but Auntie Pat was overcome with a vague hysteria and could not swallow. Her hand shook, spilling her drink onto the creamy gold carpet.

"Pat, dear," said Auntie Faye, signaling to Ravenna to fetch a rag. "Don't take on so. After all, it's been, what? Fifteen years since you last saw Vida."

"What does that matter?" Auntie Pat replied. "Elizabeth has no parents now. That's a horrible thing. You don't know what it's like, Faye. You were too busy when Mother died to let it sink in."

She turned to me, full of woe and ignoring Auntie Faye's spluttered objections. "I know how you must be suffering," she said, her voice driving me back against the cushions. "Even if no one else in this cold family understands, I do." Again she drew in closer and I thought I would suffocate in her grief.

Auntie Faye bristled with annoyance as she took the cloth Ravenna brought her and mopped the pool of sherry from the carpet. "Vida would not have liked you going on like this," she said, digging into the wet pile. She studied a tuft or two at near range. "As for Elizabeth, she's come here to live. Haven't you, Elizabeth?" she asked me without looking up from the carpet.

Not sure of anything, I managed to reply, "Yes," and Auntie Faye continued, "The money from Vida's share of Grandmother's estate will provide for her welfare for a very long time, so as you can see, Pat, everything is in order." She stopped, rocking on her heels when she caught a warning look from Uncle Niall.

"Why are you shaking your head like that, Niall? You know as well as I the money is intact. We made sure of it before Vida took off for London. It was the one piece of advice she conceded to take from us, God knows why. She never listened to anything else we told her."

Uncle Niall pinched the bridge of his nose and frowned. "There will be trouble with the money," he said.

"What do you mean?" Auntie Faye snapped. She stood up and folded the damp, sherry-soaked cloth into an angry square.

Auntie Pat sniffed. "Yes, what do you mean?" she echoed, although she hardly seemed in a state to receive further bad news. Freed for the moment from her clingy concern, I hugged a throw pillow to my chest and desperately wished all this could be over and we could be back where we started, with my mother selfishly alive. But Uncle Niall was talking and I couldn't block out his voice.

"It's Vida's will," he said. "I've been on the phone all

afternoon to London, at my own expense I might add, and there appears to be a certain clause about Elizabeth's education." He paused, as if considering how to phrase his next sentence.

Auntie Faye stood directly in front of her husband. "There's no need to speak as though we're your patients, Niall. I want to know the truth."

Bowing to his wife's request with a much-put-upon air of resignation, Uncle Niall continued, "Quite simply, Vida made a provision that if anything were to happen to her, which it now has, Elizabeth would only inherit her money if she returned to England and was enrolled in a boarding school. If she stays with us she, and we for that matter, won't get a thing until she's twenty-one."

Auntie Pat let out a mangled sort of scream. "Why would Vida have done such a cruel thing? Didn't she trust us?"

"Obviously not," replied Auntie Faye as Uncle Brian came to life and attempted to console his wife. "She must have thought we would take Elizabeth's money from her and not use it for her upkeep like we said we would."

"I never thought Vida would be so calculating," Auntie Pat said as she accepted a handkerchief from Uncle Brian.

Auntie Faye gave them both a dark look. "Then you certainly didn't know Vida."

"Well, there's no need to make a fuss," said Uncle Niall back at the cocktail cabinet. "Elizabeth will find the compounded interest alone worth having when she comes of age and decides what she wants to do.

"Another drink, Brian?"

Auntie Faye whirled around. "Are you suggesting she wait?"

Not particularly surprised by her question, Uncle Niall calmly refilled Uncle Brian's glass before asking, "Do you think boarding school would be better?"

"It's not a choice to be made that easily," Auntie Faye said. "There are issues to be argued on both sides. You can't say the money doesn't matter."

"Oh, stop!" Auntie Pat moaned. "How can you talk about money right in front of Elizabeth and with Vida in some morgue in a foreign country? What about the funeral? And looking after her things? Her clothes? I feel so cut-off. London seems the other end of creation."

"Vida's affairs were completely under the care of her lawyer," Uncle Niall assured her. "She's not in 'some morgue' as you put it. She and Miss Parker are in the Hedgeley Co-op Funeral Home and are to be cremated in two days time as directed in her will."

Auntie Pat glanced up from her handkerchief. "Cremated? They're not sending her home? How will Elizabeth be able to attend her mother's funeral?" Again she turned to me in the false belief that I could somehow help her.

"Pat, try and get a hold of yourself. The instructions in her will are plain. She had no intention of ever coming home again. And perhaps, from a professional point of view, it's for the best Elizabeth not go through the trauma of a funeral. She can remember her mother as she was when she left her a few months ago."

Uncle Niall smiled at me, pleased that the messy side of life had been taken care of, thank God, in London by my mother's lawyer, a stranger I had never known to exist before today.

"I don't care," Auntie Pat said. "The whole ruddy business sounds cold to me, what with the problem over the money and I don't know what else. Vida must have lost her mind."

"Vida always was headstrong," Auntie Faye agreed. She came and sat down between Ravenna and me. She rubbed her eyes, too tired for any further argument.

"Do you think we could have a memorial service?" Auntie Pat asked. "Perhaps next Sunday, to give Morgan and Sheena time to make plans."

"Good heavens," said Auntie Faye. "Morgan. Has anyone thought to ring Morgan?"

"I tried after London," Uncle Niall said. "But there was no reply. Would you like to tell him, Faye?"

"Yes, certainly." Auntie Faye stood up, ready to take charge again.

Halfway to the kitchen, she stopped and added, "Pat is in no condition to go back home, and we need to eat. Why doesn't someone go around to the house, find Wendy and Clare and get some Chinese food for supper? We can eat here tonight."

Uncle Niall seemed glad to take up her suggestion.

"Shall we go together, Brian? You can lock up the house then." Going for his car keys a tad eagerly, he called to Auntie Faye before leaving. "You women will be all right on your own?"

"Yes, yes," Auntie Faye said. "Let me go ring Morgan. Ravenna and Elizabeth can sit with Pat." She turned again to Auntie Pat. "Do make an effort."

When her mother was gone, Ravenna stood up and turned on several lamps. "Is there anything I can get you, Auntie Pat?" From the kitchen we could hear Auntie Faye breaking the news to her brother.

Auntie Pat shook her head. "I'm sorry to fall apart like this," she murmured. Sadly, she looked at me, as if imagining her own daughters in my position.

"It's not fair, is it?" she asked. "All of us wrapped up tight in our grief, not paying you any heed except to talk of your money. Whatever must you think of us?"

I stirred uneasily, emitting embarrassed sounds that meant, "Don't worry about me, I'm fine," but Ravenna would not accept these hedged replies.

"Elizabeth won't cry," she said.

Auntie Pat pushed herself out of the chair and went to the window. "She will," she said, opening the drapes. Lights from a cruise ship anchored in the bay twinkled with an intrusive gaiety, bringing Ravenna and me to her side. For a moment I longed to be down there with the ship, floating along with the dark, purple-black waves. I thought of the unseen passengers laughing and dancing in the ballrooms, blissfully unaware of our dreary presence as we stood above them, mournfully perched on our piece of the rock face.

Auntie Pat put her hand on my shoulder. "I'm afraid your mother and I were never close," she said. "She was always struggling to get away, as if she resented any sort of contact or concern. But that didn't mean I stopped caring for her. We were sisters. We were Haddons." She laughed; a hollow, lonely sound. "Heaven knows why we were so proud of that name. It never brought us much more than our grandmother's money. But my father believed in it. 'We are Haddons,' he would say when he wanted us to achieve more than we were able." Auntie Pat let fresh tears flow down her face with no attempt to clarify her last statement.

"You girls should stick together," she said instead, continuing to stare at the ship's lights blazing through the darkness. "Don't be like Vida and turn away from each other."

The back door slammed and Auntie Pat left off her memories, hastily drying her eyes as she closed the curtains. Wendy and Clare entered the room, their arms laden with steaming paper bags smelling of garlic and roast pork.

"That was quick," Ravenna remarked. She took some of the bags from Clare.

"Is Elizabeth's mother really dead?" Clare asked in a worried stage whisper.

"Yes, darling," replied Auntie Pat. "Say you're sorry."

"Why?"

"Because you just are, that's why."

"I'm sorry," Clare repeated, as bewildered as me.

Auntie Faye brought plates and cutlery from the kitchen, setting everything out on a card table with an exaggerated bustle and clatter while the men came in and renewed their drinks.

"What did Morgan say?" Auntie Pat asked her.

Auntie Faye stepped back to survey the results of her table setting and sighed. "Not much. But we won't think of that now. The food will grow cold."

And so the eight of us mourned my mother's passing with egg rolls and small talk. "Don't dwell on the past," advised Auntie Faye, so we stuck to the safe subjects like, wasn't this the best sweet and sour sauce we had ever tasted?

When I could only pick at my food, Auntie Faye said, "You can go to bed anytime, dear."

There was a momentary respectful silence as I stood up to leave the table and I hurried my goodnights to get away as soon as possible. But I was certain I heard the words "Vida," "will," and "boarding school" long after I had left the room, and I was disquieted by the insidious way they were spoken.

By the time I returned to bed, sleep was impossible. The heft of the thick wool blankets we used summer or winter was oppressive and I began to think in earnest of what Uncle Niall had meant about my mother's will. If I had understood correctly, the family had the choice of taking care of me until I was grown, without money, or sending me back to England and a boarding school. I wanted to stay, but I thought I also had enough wisdom to divine which course any practical adult would choose.

The summer gales had started, rattling windowpanes and tossing branches until their noise mimicked the rough sound of the sea. Kept awake by the turmoil both outside and in, I could find no earthly reason why Auntie Faye would let me stay on here with or without money. I would never have the kind of life Ravenna enjoyed. It was hopeless, and I decided to tell Ravenna how I felt while there was still time.

The house by night was full of shadow and sharp corners that made navigation difficult. I had to pass through the kitchen to get from my end of the house to Ravenna's and I was unprepared to discover her in the dark, groping along the cupboards and paneling.

"Oh!" Ravenna flattened herself against a table edge. "What are you doing up?"

"I just had to see you before I left."

"Where are you going?"

I leaned on the back of a chair for support and attempted an explanation. "You heard your father," I said. "There's no money if I stay here. It's a sure thing everyone will want me to go back to England. Maybe even by the end of the week."

The lights flickered on before Ravenna could speak.

"Girls," Auntie Faye said, standing in the doorway. "What are you doing?"

"Elizabeth thinks we don't want her to stay."

"That's ridiculous! Of course she's staying." Auntie

Faye lowered the lights and began to move around in the near dark, tidying up the stale remains of our Chinese meal and her confusion. Ravenna joined her in collecting the unused packets of soy sauce and mustard.

"I won't make-believe the money doesn't count," Auntie Faye continued. "It does. But not enough to be wasted on some boarding school we don't know the least thing about. Anyway, your father and I have come to a very satisfactory conclusion about Elizabeth's future that will solve everything."

"What conclusion?" I asked, thinking the future sounded centuries away.

"Not now," Auntie Faye said, drying her hands. She put the soy sauce in the refrigerator. "We'll talk in the morning. It's bedtime now, for both of you. Ravenna is leading story hour on the children's ward tomorrow morning. Sleep well."

I nodded, thinking my whole life sounded like story hour on the children's ward. Auntie Faye turned out the light and led Ravenna back to her room. I watched them go; content at knowing I would be part of yet another morning. Already my heart was feeling lighter, soaring away from my mother for good.

Chapter Six

The next morning, Auntie Faye laid her plans before me as though delivering a thin-shelled egg that needed special handling.

"None of this will be easy," she said. "But with a little effort on your part, Elizabeth, we will manage. We will manage splendidly." She poured herself another cup of tea and gave me a biscuit sandwiched with raspberry jam before imparting the essence of her idea.

"I know you won't appreciate the finer points at this stage," she said, "because young people rarely do. But if you were to be enrolled in a special secretarial course they have at Whitworth's Business Academy after the holidays, you could be out working by the time you were, say, seventeen. Earning money," she said to my stare of complete bafflement. "Money that could pay back your keep here and perhaps give you a small bit to put aside. That way, when you reach your majority, you won't have to go into your mother's inheritance until you actually need it." She set her cup down and beamed at me. "Isn't that a nice, sensible plan?"

It certainly was if I had any intention of becoming a secretary, a career I knew from my mother's constant refrain that she would rather die than be one. Fate having granted her wish, I was now doomed to take her reluctant place.

"Are you listening, Elizabeth?" asked Auntie Faye.

"Yes, Auntie."

Auntie Faye sighed, something she was rapidly turning into a habit. "Your mother should have become a secretary," she said. "It would have saved us all a lot of worry."

Ravenna had slept in a little and she came to the table with her hair tousled and her eyelids red. I wondered if she had been crying, but Auntie Faye appeared not to see anything amiss.

"Toast or cornflakes, dear?" she asked, rising to fill Ravenna's order.

"Cornies will be okay." Ravenna looked at me from under her lashes. "Did you sleep?"

"I tried to." I watched Auntie Faye give Ravenna her cereal, and added, "I have to be a secretary."

Auntie Faye brought milk and sugar to the table and said, "Elizabeth, you don't have to be anything. It is a suggestion. You mustn't feel we are pressuring you."

Ravenna poured milk into a bowl and waited for her cornflakes to go soggy. "You'd make a good secretary," she said. "You're clever. You're the bookish one in the family." Her words carried a degree of respect.

I frowned at the tablecloth. "Bookish" was limp hair and wool skirts and described me to a T.

Having exhausted what was in truth a very boring topic, Ravenna began to eat, asking between mouthfuls, "What have you decided about the memorial service, Mummy? Are we having one?"

Auntie Faye pretended to be absorbed with sorting laundry. "No," she said, intent on the heel of a sock. "With Christmas so soon it just isn't fair to give Vicar the extra workload. Besides, Morgan and Sheena can't leave the farm and that doesn't leave many people who remember Vida kindly." Again she sighed, a long, drawn-out attempt to fend off further probing.

"I think Auntie Pat would like one," Ravenna persisted.

"Then let Auntie Pat organize it!" Auntie Faye gripped the handles of her basket while Ravenna rolled her eyes at me. After a moment Auntie Faye cooled down enough to say, "Pat is too sentimental for her own good. She should realize our job is to carry on. We have to plan for the future and send Elizabeth to secretarial school." With new resolve, Auntie Faye straightened her back and swept the floor.

Ravenna watched her for a second. "Maybe you could ask Vicar to add a bit to his regular sermon," she said. "Then everyone would be happy."

Auntie Faye kept sweeping. "Possibly. Perhaps along the lines of: 'And we all want to give the families of the deceased our deepest sympathies at their recent loss.'

"I don't think Vicar would mind, but I do hate to bother him right now with the holidays so close. Although he is just the person to ask for a reference if we want to get Elizabeth a scholarship into Whitworth's."

Ravenna turned to me. "Do you want to go to Whitworth's?"

"Not really."

"Elizabeth!" Auntie Faye put down her broom. "I thought it was all settled. Surely you don't want to go to boarding school with absolute strangers!"

"I don't see why I can't just go to regular school here," I mumbled.

Auntie Faye tried to appear patient. "You can't because your mother made it impossible for us to support you without money. Do you understand what I mean?"

I looked at Ravenna, knowing very well what her mother meant.

"I'd hate to be a secretary," Ravenna said, but Auntie Faye's glare made her hastily withdraw the comment.

"Don't interfere," she said. "Vida set this whole thing into motion and now it's up to me to solve a difficulty I don't like any better than the rest of you. But there it is. Vida behaved irresponsibly and I must do my best. And not for the first time."

A knock at the front door relieved her for the moment of her unasked-for responsibilities and she left in a hurry to answer it. When she returned, she brought with her a look loaded with caution and a small, round woman with a spray of silk orchids pinned to her lapel. The flowers were starting to wilt in the humidity.

"Elizabeth," Auntie Faye said, "this is my friend, Mattie

Grateful. We went to school together."

"You little lambkin," said Mattie, making a beeline for me. "I've been worried sick about you." Without giving me a chance to respond, Mattie turned back to Auntie Faye. "I just stopped by to offer my condolences," she said. "So sad about Vida. But as my gran used to say, she made her own bed." Mattie helped herself to a biscuit. "Your baking is still the best, Faye. I don't know how you do it all. Mind if I take this with me? I'm off to visit the Burley girl. She's just had twins if you can believe it! You'll be stopping by the house for Christmas?"

Auntie Faye was about to speak when another interruption at the front door called her away.

"It's death," Mattie Grateful said cheerfully, helping herself to a second biscuit. "Brings people out of the house, it does." Brimming with curiosity, Mattie chewed her biscuit and peeped into the hallway. "I think your Auntie Pat is here," she said, her mouth still full. "Well, I'll be going. Don't bother seeing me out, girls. I know the way. Goodbye, lambkin!" She left via the back door with much the same flurry as she had entered.

"Where's Mattie?" asked Auntie Faye when she came back with a much subdued Auntie Pat.

"She left," Ravenna said.

Auntie Pat studied the plate of biscuits with a doleful expression and said, "I expect she wants us to go for Christmas."

"And why not? We can't send the whole town into

mourning because our sister dies in a foreign country."

Auntie Pat sat down at the table with Ravenna and me. "The Gratefuls are so loud," she said. "Going to their place right on the heels of Vida's memorial service seems insensitive, don't you think?"

"There isn't going to be a memorial service."

"Faye! You can't do that. It would be unforgivable." She sat back, unable to continue.

Auntie Faye waved her hand in annoyance. "Don't start your melodramatics with me, Pat. You haven't a clue what a night I've had worrying about poor Elizabeth and I'm in no mood to justify myself."

I squirmed at the idea of causing any more upset than I had, but neither aunt took any notice.

"What's the harm in a simple, tasteful service?"

"There isn't time, that's what," Auntie Faye said, her voice rising into the higher octaves. "Vicar is up to his ears organizing the Christmas festivities and I can't ask him to stop and write a eulogy for a tramp."

There. The word was out at last. Auntie Faye must have been holding it in for a very long time, longer than she could actually bear. Ravenna went to the rubbish and tipped out the last of her cornflakes.

"I'm sorry you feel that way," Auntie Pat said at last. Standing to leave, she mechanically kissed Ravenna and then me good-bye, and then, like Mattie Grateful, she found her own way to the door.

Auntie Faye let her get as far as the washer before she

said, "Pat, come back here and sit down this instant."

Auntie Pat waited for one face-saving minute before meekly returning to the table. When she was seated again, Auntie Faye said, "This is no time to quarrel. There are far more important things to consider than ourselves and a silly, useless memorial service."

Auntie Pat nodded. "You could be right."

"Of course I am," Auntie Faye said. "Now I do think you should go home and have a nice lie down and forget all about this nonsense. Sound good?"

This time Auntie Pat let her sister accompany her to the door but when Auntie Faye returned, her displeasure was written all over her face. "Excuse me, girls," she said, "but I must lie down myself. I don't think I can take another minute. Ravenna, don't forget about story hour, will you?"

Ravenna shook her head. "No, Mummy."

When Auntie Faye was gone, Ravenna leaned toward me. "Maybe a secretarial course won't be so bad. At any rate you'll know what you'll be doing in life."

"Taking dictation and answering phones? What kind of life is that?"

"A real, grown-up kind of life. Better than story hour and endless community teas for the elderly."

"But, but…." I couldn't finish.

"But what?"

"But the ballet and the voice lessons and all the wonderful things you do. They're real. They're exciting and fun. I'll never have any of them if I go to Whitworth's."

"Who wants any of that?"

"I do."

"You wouldn't if you'd had them since you were four years old. Listen, I wasn't good at anything else and I'm not particularly good at any of the things Mummy pushes me toward now, either."

My disbelief made her get up and twirl around the room. "You still don't understand, do you?" she asked.

I shook my head.

"Look, I go through the motions, but that doesn't make me a dancer. Anyone can point her toes and jump around, but talent is an entirely different matter altogether. And I haven't got it.

"Anyway, can you honestly think of Mummy wanting me to end up on the stage? She'd be horrified. To her, this is busy work. A hobby to keep me out of mischief until I get married. No," she said, going to the sink and roughly rinsing out the breakfast dishes. "What she wants for me is a good, solid marriage. Just like hers."

Ravenna turned off the water just in time before Auntie Faye rejoined us. "I thought you were lying down," she said too quickly, as if she feared her mother may have caught her in the act of complaining.

But Auntie Faye hadn't heard a thing. Instead she said, "I couldn't rest. Such a to-do this has all become." She held her hand out to me. "You do realize it's your welfare we care about, don't you, Elizabeth?"

"Yes, Auntie," I said, taking her hand and keeping my

eyes on Ravenna's back.

Auntie Faye sat down and changed her slippers for a pair of shoes. "Whitworth's is a wonderful school. The woman who runs it is a patient of your Uncle Niall's. Everyone, just everyone who's been there has turned out well."

I tried to put some enthusiasm into my nodded agreement and Auntie Faye turned her attention back to Ravenna. "Let's all try to smile, dear. Remember, it's nearly Christmas."

"Yes, Mummy." Obediently, Ravenna made the effort to play her required role and once again the pendulum swung back to something resembling harmony.

The next few days were rife with preparations for the holidays and attempts to bring my wardrobe up to scratch for Whitworth's. I would be entering the school on a scholarship in early February, the same month as my fifteenth birthday. As a uniform was not required, Auntie Faye now had the added task of weeding through my limited stock of clothing to find whatever could be salvaged.

"I suppose some of this could go to the New Year's Mission Society sale," she said, holding up an absurdly small pair of pajamas. She tilted her head to one side as if measuring me. "What about that green dress Ravenna gave you? I never see you in it any more. Doesn't it fit?"

Seizing my opportunity, I said, "No, it's far too small."

"Well, fold it up. There's still some use in it for someone."

In this way a pattern of sorts was established. Daily, I

rid myself of all my loathsome clothing under the guise of "helping out." "For the Mission Society," I'd say, bringing Auntie Faye another blouse or skirt, at the same time feeling not entirely blameless when I thought of children in the equatorial regions sweating in my cast-off tweeds.

Auntie Faye was too busy to notice anything corrupt in my philanthropy. By the time Christmas Eve arrived, she was glad to spend the night quietly at home. It had rained all that day, giving Auntie Pat the excuse to forego bringing Wendy, Clare, and Uncle Brian over to visit us. "We will see each other tomorrow as usual," she had told Auntie Faye over the telephone.

Ravenna and I were in the kitchen making a frill of gold foil for the fruitcake we were taking to the Grateful's party when she rang. We stopped to listen, for Auntie Pat had not spoken to us since the day she learned there was to be no memorializing my mother.

"I'm so glad you've seen reason over Vida's service," Auntie Faye said sweetly into the phone. "And the Gratefuls will be so, well, *grateful*." She laughed and I realized this must be an old joke. "Why don't you come here first?

"Right-o. We'll try for ten. Happy Christmas, dear." Auntie Faye hung up the phone with a flourish; not all of her plans had been thwarted by my mother.

Ravenna and I finished our frill without comment and then went to sit with Uncle Niall and the scraggly, expensive tree he had brought home for us. The heat was causing the pine needles to drop off one by one and gaping bare patches were already in evidence, making the whole odd experience of a summer Christmas even more peculiar to me. I was, however, heartened by the stack of gifts I saw labeled with my name. Despite their ominous lumpiness, arousing my suspicions they contained replacements for everything I had given away, I couldn't resist pulling on a ribbon or two.

"Nothing is to be opened until morning!" Auntie Faye warned, playing the wag as she brought in a fresh pot of tea. She took Uncle Niall's newspaper away and gave him a cup and saucer to hold. "What a lovely night," she said.

"It's too hot," answered Ravenna. She stretched out on the floor, propping her chin in her hands to stare at the Christmas tree lights flash on and off.

"I wasn't referring to the weather," Auntie Faye said. "I meant how nice it was to have us all home for once. Of course I miss Pat and her family, but this is quite cozy." She settled back in her chair, cradling her teacup.

Ravenna turned over onto her back. "Maybe we could skip the Gratefuls for a change."

Auntie Faye seemed surprised. "Going to the Gratefuls isn't a social occasion, Ravenna. It's an old family tradition that would upset Mattie terribly if we didn't participate. It would be pure selfishness to stay away."

Ravenna glanced my way. "Mummy and Mattie Grateful played on the same netball team, so every year we do the same old thing: stand around in her garden eating wet peanuts and broken potato crisps while the men get drunk."

"Really, Ravenna!"

Ravenna yawned. "It's the truth."

"That is quite enough," snapped Auntie Faye. "You are doing your best to upset me and you are positively destroying Elizabeth's morale. Just look at her."

I sat up quickly to demonstrate how firmly my morale was intact. I positively beamed. The last thing I wanted was to be blamed for ruining Christmas more than my mother had.

"We have always spent Christmas with the Gratefuls and I see no reason why this year should be any different. Vida would have wanted us to enjoy ourselves. She was never one to begrudge a good time."

I crouched beside the red and green unopened parcels, feeling a bit like one of them myself, and waited for something to happen. But Auntie Faye fell silent with her tea, Uncle Niall resumed his newspaper, and Ravenna closed her eyes. I concentrated on looking deep into the heart of a midnight blue glass bubble, and I remember thinking, *this is just the calm before the storm.* And I wondered what I meant.

Chapter Seven

One year later, we were still victims of habit, compelled to spend our Christmas mornings with the Gratefuls. Indeed, the time between holidays passed so quickly it was as if some bizarre stroke of misfortune had imprisoned us for eternity in their overgrown, midge-ridden garden.

But that particular Christmas was to be the last of its innocent kind, for that was the year my carefully nurtured life as a "Whitworth's girl" shattered apart. Ravenna decided to get married, and she never thought to tell me first.

Instead, I was asked to stand with the rest of Mattie Grateful's unsuspecting guests when Auntie Faye made the sudden, and quite startling, announcement.

"It gives me the greatest pleasure in the world," she said, "to share with you the engagement of our daughter, Ravenna Marie, to Mr. Alan Trask." Auntie Faye paused, and then no power on earth could have prevented her from adding, "Alan Trask of the supermarket empire, that is."

At first there was a rumble of emotion like the pulling back of a great, strong wave, and then the voices swelled to a crest of excitement Auntie Faye rode like a queen. Any misgivings she may have harbored prior to this moment were swept away forever. And I had never even known Ravenna's middle name was "Marie."

But none of Mattie's tipsy friends cared about that. It was all, "When's the wedding?" and "Where's the honeymoon?" and I wished I were a million miles away.

Ravenna lowered her eyes and mumbled bashful answers the women in the party swooped to gather to themselves for late night contemplation. Even Wendy, who earlier had done her best to fade into the background, now lit up with a twist of malicious envy in her smile. I was the only one, it appeared, anxious for the ground to reach up and bury me, or at least to rise high enough for me to dig my heels in and stop these unwanted changes. Ravenna was leaving me and I reacted like an idiot; I ran to the farthest end of the Grateful's Victorian garden, to a place hidden and used for burning.

My heart fell out onto the ashes generated from a hundred past winters. Every ounce of my strength went to resist this interloper, this Alan Trask of the supermarket chains. Woven through my pain was the thought of Ravenna's deliberate silence, excluding and bypassing me for the dubious glory of shining in front of a gathering of aged colonials.

There must have been signs this was coming. There must have been clues strewn all over the house to warn me, but I had been too busy with exams and too anxious to please Auntie Faye to see any life but my own. Thinking back, I could just remember a dinner dance Ravenna had waltzed off to, her dress and hair closely supervised by Auntie Faye before she was allowed to leave and make her mother proud. That was followed by a party in the city, later written up in the social pages of the newspaper and saved by Auntie Faye with similar trophies. The memories began to click: the expensive cars in our driveway; the whispered conversations outside my window; the boxes of cut flowers arriving on weekends from "nobody." Alan Trask had fallen in love with Ravenna and I had been too absorbed with the "Whitworth Way" of dictation and basic accounting to take in the world around me.

"How could you stand keeping it a secret?"

I turned as Clare and the Grateful's Labrador-cross came snuffling up to me, both full of what seemed like wily, ingratiating tricks for claiming undeserved attention. "Easy," I said, wiping my eyes. "Nobody told me so I could hardly give the game away if I tried."

Clare didn't look as if she believed me and she began to torment the dog, Rip; kicking him away and then calling him back for more of the same. "Well, I think it's fantastic," she said. "Though it would have been better if Alan Trask was here in person. Where is he, anyway?"

"How should I know? Probably counting his supermarkets."

Clare was in awe. "Really? How many has he got?" When I didn't answer, she closed her eyes with a dreamy expression on her face. "Just think. They met at my house." She opened her eyes and glanced back to Ravenna's circle of admirers. "Ravenna has always been the lucky one," she said. "Here she comes now. Isn't her dress gorgeous?"

Ravenna's flowered voile skirts lifted and floated behind her in the breeze as she picked her way across the grass to us. For a long minute she stood apart, studying the ashes before saying, "You think I'm mad, don't you?"

The question was meant for me and trying to appear aloof and mature, I shook my head. "No, but you could have given me some kind of warning. I'm not a child. I wouldn't have spoiled your surprise."

Ravenna continued to stare at the ashes, and to fill the awkward space, I said, "So how long has this been going on?" I noticed her left hand was still bare of an engagement ring.

Ravenna followed my eyes and flinched. "Oh, not very long. Just since last night. Mummy knew first, then Daddy. I was the last to find out."

"You were the last?"

There was no time for her to explain when Wendy strolled up in search of Clare. "I guess I should congratulate you or something," she said to Ravenna.

"Thanks." Humbly, Ravenna bent her head.

"Come on, Clare," Wendy said. "Dad's had enough of this place and wants to go home."

Clare tossed the dog a stick. "Hang on," she said, watching him bound after it. "I want to know if we get to be bridesmaids." She turned a face filled with expectation to Ravenna, but the question seemed to puzzle our cousin.

"If you like," Ravenna replied, but Wendy made a face and started to drag Clare back toward the house and the sound of boozy Christmas carols.

"Wendy's jealous," I said when they were gone, wondering if I was, too.

"What about?"

I watched Wendy and Clare leaving with their parents. Auntie Pat hadn't been very friendly to us all day and it didn't seem as if she was going to stop to say good-bye to us now. "Wendy wants to be you," I said with a catch in my voice.

"What drivel. Who would want to be me? Why, I've hardly had a chance to breathe for myself and now that I'm getting married...." Her voice trailed off and her expression grew more serious. "Doesn't that sound weird?" she asked. "Getting married?"

"Ravenna! Ravenna, Elizabeth! Over here," Auntie Faye called, beckoning with her handbag to make us hurry.

"Now what does she want?" Ravenna asked, but I had nothing to offer and we returned to the house side by side in silence.

"We have to leave," Auntie Faye said, leading us to the long tables edging the garden where she began to cover cakes with waxed paper. "There is too much to do to stand around here all day if we're to get ready for a summer wedding."

"I don't mind if I have a winter wedding," Ravenna said. She put the wrapped cakes into a hamper. "What does it matter?"

"Winter weather won't make for good photos, dear."

Auntie Faye continued rounding up all the bits and pieces she had brought to enliven Mattie's party before she then rushed our farewells to the hostess. "I'll ring about the dresses," she told Mattie. "With any luck you can start sewing by the end of the week."

To my mind, Mattie took the news rather sadly, though whether she was depressed by the amount of sewing Auntie Faye was assigning her, or simply reflecting on marriage in general, it was difficult to say.

Uncle Niall was waiting for us in the car. "Ready?" he asked as we clambered inside. "Run up plenty of bills with Mattie? Had a good natter with the girls?" He snorted. "The way you women carry on you'd think there never had been a wedding since the beginning of time."

"Please, Niall. Don't start complaining," said Auntie Faye. "This wedding is an investment in Ravenna's future and we don't want Alan thinking we're too shabby to give her a proper send-off. Be thankful you only have to go through it the once."

Ravenna leaned over the front seat, her head between her parents. "What if Elizabeth gets married?"

Auntie Faye turned and gave her a sour look. "Elizabeth will be too busy with her career to contemplate marriage for a long time, Ravenna. Don't go putting unsuitable ideas into the child's head."

Lately, Auntie Faye had resorted to wearing glasses whenever she felt particularly annoyed and she now took the silver-wired frames out of their case and clamped them onto her nose. Bespectacled and poker-backed, she was not a force to be taken lightly, although Uncle Niall did venture to ask as he parked outside the front door, "When's dinner?"

Auntie Faye adjusted her glasses. "Soon. The roast has been in the oven all morning. I thought it best if Ravenna had an early meal before seeing Alan this evening." At the mention of her fiancé's name, Ravenna's smile became less assured but Auntie Faye was steeped in private visions of a Hollywood wedding and took no notice. "Pink would be nice for the bridesmaids," she continued. "It's more flattering against the skin than some of the strange colors they're using these days. What do you think, Ravenna? Do you like pink?"

Uncle Niall rolled his eyes.

"Pink's fine," Ravenna said, letting herself out of the car. Auntie Faye opened her door more slowly while she instructed me to remind her to ring Mattie later to search out all the pink fabric in town.

"Why everything has to be closed tomorrow is beyond me," she said. "We'll lose an entire day's shopping. Never mind, we'll make lists."

Still talking to herself, Auntie Faye left Uncle Niall to put the car away. "Oh, the newspapers!" she screeched, frightening him to a stop. "We must contact them as soon as possible if they haven't found out already."

"Weddings," said Uncle Niall in the same dismal tone he used for anything remotely connected to a good time.

Christmas dinner consisted of roast beef and potatoes, applesauce, and two kinds of salad, the same meal we had eaten for Christmas the previous year. But because the kitchen needed to be cleared in record time for Alan Trask's first official holiday visit, I was scarcely able to take more than a few mouthfuls before Auntie Faye whisked each course from the table. For dessert I had to be satisfied with a slice of date loaf outside on the back steps and even then Auntie Faye wouldn't let me have a plate.

I don't know who was the more nervous, Ravenna or Auntie Faye, but Uncle Niall refused to change out of his slippers for anyone. While Auntie Faye began an early spring-clean, he settled down in the lounge to read the latest surgical reports from Australia. It wasn't until I walked past Ravenna's room on the way to complete an errand for Auntie Faye that I understood the tempest we were in.

"You've got to help me!" Ravenna wailed as I glanced through her open door. Discarded dresses were thrown down at random; the shoes she wore with them scattered and dumped on their sides. "I can't find anything, *anything* worth wearing!"

I made some room to sit down on the bed and held up one of Ravenna's best blouses. "What's wrong with this?" I fingered the intricate embroidery on the mandarin collar and pushed aside the misery I felt at the thought of her leaving.

Ravenna groaned and pulled at the heated rollers in her hair. "That horrible thing? You can have it if you want. I hate it."

It was almost brand new and not the sort of thing Auntie Faye usually pulled from Ravenna's closet for me. I folded the blouse on my lap before she could reconsider the offer and mustered the courage to ask, "When's the great man arriving?"

Ravenna gave me a blank look and started to brush the curls out of her hair.

"You know, Alan Old-Money Trask."

"Don't be awful," Ravenna said, dotting on foundation with a shaky hand. "It's not like you."

"What is like me?" I was truly curious but Ravenna just said, "Alan will be here in twenty minutes and I haven't one decent outfit to show my face in."

I looked at the piles of clothing littering the bed and floor. "All this and you can't find one thing to wear?" I wondered what else she would hate in the next few minutes.

"You don't understand. They're too—young. Alan is very sophisticated. Now that we're engaged, I can't keep meeting him looking like a baby."

"I remember when you didn't want to meet him ever. Not even in a new blue and white summer suit."

Abruptly, Ravenna came to sit beside me. She slumped forward, her head on her knees. "That day at the beach. It was fun, wasn't it?"

"I wanted it to last forever."

She sat up. "There'll be other times. And after I'm married, I can do things for you. You can come to my house whenever you like, perhaps after your classes at Whitworth's, and meet people, get out in the world. I know it will be rough stuck here with Mummy, but she leaves you alone pretty much."

I could hear the telephone ringing and Auntie Faye's rush to answer it.

Impatient with her emotions, Ravenna stood and went to her mirror as if for solace. "I know none of this makes any sense," she said before I could speak, "but you don't need this kind of opportunity to be someone. This marriage is the best thing that will ever happen to me. I'm not clever enough to stay in school and I'm not talented enough to sing and dance my way to the top, whatever that is. This is my big chance." She spoke so bitterly I thought she would start crying in a minute, but she rapidly relaxed her face when Auntie Faye tapped on the door.

"What a mess!" she exclaimed with a laugh meant, I supposed, to put us at ease. "I'm sorry to tell you it's been for nothing."

From the mirror, Ravenna gazed at her mother's reflection. "Nothing?"

"Sorry, dear, but poor Alan can't join us tonight after all." Auntie Faye sighed. "It's business."

"Business?" Ravenna's mild echo was unsettling.

"Don't take it like that," said Auntie Faye, as if Ravenna had a choice. "He was most apologetic, but there's someone arrived from Japan. Alan has to see the man before tomorrow when he leaves for Timaru."

Auntie Faye gave Ravenna a bright smile and started to re-hang her clothes. She stopped when she saw the blouse on my lap. "What's that?"

"Ravenna gave it to me."

Auntie Faye returned to her task. "Oh, well," she said from inside the closet. "If she knows what's she's doing." Ravenna inclined her head and Auntie Faye got back to her version of work ethics. "This is what it means to marry a successful man, dear. If you want the financial benefits, you will have to be prepared for small sacrifices." She dusted off several pairs of Ravenna's shoes with her apron and lined them up beneath the rows of now neatly organized skirts and floor-length dresses. "Coming out for a cup of tea, then?"

"In a bit."

"Good girl. That's the ticket, don't brood. It's not healthy."

Ravenna waited for her mother to leave before turning to me with a relieved smile on her face. "The price of freedom," she said with an exaggerated sense of the dramatic. She then fell face down on her bed and laughed until the tears came.

Auntie Faye made sure Ravenna used that freedom to good advantage. The following day, after Uncle Niall had left us for the golf course, she called an emergency meeting at the kitchen table.

"Start writing," she said, handing us each paper and a

pencil stub. "Flowers. Invitations. Ring the paper to put the notice in. Talk to Mattie. You didn't remind me, Elizabeth," she added, full of reproof. "What else? Choosing a pattern and fabric to give to Mattie. Book the restaurant for the reception. I thought that new marina place was the nicest choice in the end. Oh, rings! We mustn't forget to pick up your engagement ring, Ravenna."

Ravenna began to draw a lop-sided house on her paper. "No, Mummy. We won't forget."

Auntie Faye looked at me. "Alan is having his grandmother's opals altered to fit Ravenna's finger. Isn't that nice?"

"If you like used jewelry," I said, wondering what Ravenna thought to be on the receiving end of second-hand goods for a change, but Auntie Faye didn't hear me and was busy concentrating on her list.

"Think," she prompted.

"I can't," I said. "I've never helped plan a wedding before."

"That's the trouble," agreed Auntie Faye. "None of us have."

Ravenna added trees to her drawing.

Ticking off items from a separate list she had made earlier, Auntie Faye was in a world of her own. "A seafood buffet would be best, with a lamb curry at the end for those who want something a little more solid."

Feeling I was expected to comment in some way, I asked, "When's the big day? Or is it a secret?"

Ravenna stopped her doodling. "I don't know," she said. She set her pencil down and tore the paper in two.

"It will have to be soon," Auntie Faye said.

"Why?"

"You want the sun to shine, don't you?"

"Do I?"

"Don't be cynical, dear," Auntie Faye said. "You have to stay happy. It's a bride's duty."

We stayed at the table doing our best to stay happy for another half hour before Auntie Faye said there was nothing more we could accomplish until Alan Trask set the date and the shops opened. Alan Trask proved more rewarding than the shops, however, when he later rang Ravenna from Wellington, over four hundred miles away. He was in the middle of entertaining another party from Japan, but he had a quick ten minutes to spare for her.

Ravenna came off the phone and told us Alan wanted the wedding in the first few days of February. "The third, if we can manage it," she said, an apology in her voice.

"Excellent," said Auntie Faye. "That will give us five weeks. Heaps of time for things to fall into place."

I asked to be excused and went to my room. I tried to read, but couldn't make sense of the first line. The words "five weeks" drummed through my head. Five weeks until Ravenna left. I slouched on the floor and brooded regardless of Auntie Faye's insistence we remain happy. Maybe it wasn't bad luck, I thought, to brood if you were just the wedding attendant.

At the end of a week memorable for the largest shopping spree Auntie Faye had ever indulged in, we finally met with Alan Trask as a family. We were going out to dinner with him and even when Ravenna chose a dress for me far nicer than her own, nothing had prepared me for the formality and elegance of the occasion.

The restaurant Alan eventually decided upon was as luxurious as anything displayed in one of Auntie Faye's magazines. Crystal chandeliers reflected light back down onto the sheen of the damask table linen and the silver cutlery was almost too heavy to lift. Auntie Faye was over the moon with happiness.

Bemused and remote, Alan Trask was something of a disappointment. For one thing, he had aged over the year since I had last seen him at Auntie Pat's barbecue. For another, he was completely devoid of conversation. Of course, he knew all the right ways to flatter Auntie Faye, listening graciously to her ceaseless prattle about the upcoming wedding without a single yawn. I found him utterly boring.

Auntie Faye, a shiny bundle of nerves in turquoise shantung, obviously did not share my opinion and all but called him "Sir Alan" whenever she addressed him. Ravenna, not a hair out of place, flashed her now-altered opals when required and deferred all questions to her mother; while Uncle Niall just seemed glad he wasn't picking up the tab.

"It was simply the loveliest evening," Auntie Faye gushed afterwards to Mattie Grateful. We were with Wendy and Clare for the final fittings of the bridesmaid dresses. Mattie wanted to know if she was to sew velvet or watered silk sashes, but Auntie Faye wasn't quite finished describing the previous night's menu and when she began on the dessert—profiteroles doused in apricot brandy—Wendy pushed me to the hall outside Mattie's bedroom and told me to be at the cliffs by her house in the morning.

"I might not be able to get away," I told her. "I have to finish writing Ravenna's thank you cards."

"Try." She had put some funny color rinse through her hair, upsetting Auntie Faye because she now clashed with the delicate shade of baby pink we had been modeling for weeks. "You remember the place," she continued. "We went there with Ravenna that time."

Clare padded over to us in her slip. "I want to go, too."

Wendy glared at her, and then shrugged. "Just be there," she said to me.

The next morning I told Auntie Faye I would be late home from the post office. "Be back for lunch," she said, busy with the wine list for the reception.

I took my usual route to the post office, dropped off the most recent of Ravenna's ghostwritten thanks for the sheets, towels, and coffee makers, and then cut through the un-fenced properties that led to Auntie Pat's house. Without going as far as the house, I found my way through the familiar tunnel of tree ferns and gorse that brought me to the grassy hills by the beach. The day was hotter than predicted, a sign Auntie Faye took as felicitous for the wedding and by the time I had climbed to the ledge and the waterfall my clothes stuck to my back.

"What a terrible place to meet," I complained.

Wendy and Clare sat at opposite ends of the ledge. "I think it's quite apt," Wendy said.

"What for?"

"To talk about this ludicrous wedding."

The sun in my eyes, I squinted down at the beach and realized the "waterfall" was simply an oversized drainage pipe. The water splashed down to the sand where a few girls in bikinis were attempting tans, their numbers matched by a fleet of white-sailed skiffs along the horizon. "Well, make it quick. I have to be home for lunch."

Wendy bit her lip and cast a sideways glance at Clare. "Haven't you wondered why Auntie Faye is in such a hurry to marry off Ravenna?"

"Use your head. The reason is obvious. He's a good catch. Though he is busy," I added. "Don't be shocked if he cancels at the last minute in favor of a meeting with the export union."

"Really?" Clare rustled uneasily, fear troubling her features. "Do you think he might call it off? After we have our dresses and everything?"

"Sorry, no such luck. Auntie Faye would sooner be run over by a truck."

Wendy regarded us coolly. She paused for maximum effect and then said, "She'll wish she had been after everyone hears the news."

"What news?"

"About Ravenna. She's pregnant. And it isn't Alan Trask's, 'of the supermarket empire, that is,' either."

Clare and I both looked at her and then I started to laugh. "Don't be stupid," I said. "You made me come all the way up here for that?"

Wendy crossed her arms. "Don't you believe me?"

"Of course not. The idea is, well, it's just silly."

"I don't believe you, either," Clare said, staunchly behind me.

Wendy's grin grew colder. "You're as bad as each other," she said softly. "You're both so thrilled to be included in Ravenna's latest spectacle you can't see a thing."

For a minute all I could see was Wendy's unevenly dyed hair and her empty, in-the-know smirk. She reminded me so strongly of Lily Parker I wanted to hit her. "That isn't true," I said. "None of this is. And I'm not just 'included' as you put it. Ravenna wants me there."

"Because once upon a time she put some old furniture in your room? Or she gave you some old clothes? As far as Ravenna is concerned, you might as well be as dead as your mother. She laughs at you. She laughs at all of us!"

"That isn't true," I repeated.

Wendy shrugged again and a sudden cold breeze flew up off the sea toward us, making Clare huddle closer to the rocks. I kept telling myself Wendy had dyed her brain at the same time as her hair. What on earth was wrong with her?

"Listen," I said at last, finally able to find my voice. "If you're trying to cause trouble—and I don't know why you would do that—just don't."

"Don't cause trouble for Auntie Faye, you mean?" Wendy shouted. "Don't make people talk?"

Clare and I started to answer back at the same time until I heard my voice climb over hers and crack, finishing with, "You don't know anything!"

But Wendy wouldn't stop. Placing her face close to mine, she yelled, "This whole thing is sick—it's revolting! Always it's Ravenna. Always we put on the act that we absolutely adore Ravenna. Ravenna this, Ravenna that—and she's this total fraud—"

"No!" Clare cried out so loudly the gulls flying overhead were startled into silence. "No," plain, pale, skinny little Clare repeated more quietly. "Don't say those things. You shouldn't be so mean when there's going to be a lovely wedding and, and everything."

Filled with spite, Wendy grabbed her sister by the shoulders. "Stay out of it," she warned.

"No, I won't," Clare said. She hesitated and then gave Wendy a resentful push forward, something she shouldn't have done.

I tried to intervene, but I was too slow. In a fit of mindless fury, Wendy pinched and shook Clare's shoulders, hard. "It's always Ravenna, always what she wants!" she screamed, her feet slipping in the loose stones. "I hate the way we cater to her. I hate her!"

Clare's teeth chattered together as her head bounced

back and forth between shakes and I couldn't just stand there and watch any longer.

"Cut it out," I ordered, acutely aware of the lack of authority in my voice. "Cut it out, Wendy," I said, wringing her arm, tearing at her shirt, feeling as heavy and slow as if I were ensnared in a bad dream.

With one last, vindictive shove, Wendy suddenly let go and turned violently away. Confused at her release, Clare stumbled, lost her balance, regained it, and then fell backward over the ledge. Her head twisted to one side, she slid down the wet embankment, letting out a sharp, frightened scream as her legs flew over her head, accelerating a grotesque somersault that finished with her splayed against the rocks and trees over twenty feet below.

"It's always Ravenna!" Wendy screamed over and over to the sky, her back turned to me.

My stomach tightened when I saw Clare laying there, her small face scored with blackish red gashes. Surely she was dead, but then I heard a faint whimpering, "Don't tell, Elizabeth. Don't tell Auntie Faye...."

The sea air dried the sweat off my back and I shuddered, sensing something huge and made of darkness had come at last for us.

Chapter Eight

The hospital waiting room was too small to contain the full extent of Auntie Pat's distress. She moaned and cried and shut her ears to Auntie Faye's vigorous appeals for reasonable behavior. She could not possibly believe that Uncle Niall would see to Clare and we would all be home in time for lunch. After two hours she turned her back to burrow more comfortably into her conviction that things would only get worse, exasperating Auntie Faye to almost a minute of hard-pressed silence.

Three chairs away, Wendy sat expressionless, flipping through a *Newsweek* and tapping her foot on the floor until Auntie Faye begged her to kindly please stop; couldn't she see she was driving her mother mad?

And me, I thought, unable to shake the image of Clare twisted and broken like the tree roots. She's driving me mad, too.

"What happened?" Auntie Pat cried out to me again. She ignored the stares from another, quieter family patiently sharing what was left of the waiting room with us. "What happened?" She threw me a look so anguished I ducked with guilt and fixed my mind on the dried sand on my ankles and a pine needle stuck in the buckle of my shoe.

"I told you," Wendy said in a flat voice, turning the pages of her magazine in search of a more interesting story. "She fell. She's always been clumsy."

"But what were you doing up there? Why were you there?"

Auntie Faye sighed. "The girls were just having a little get-together. They were discussing the wedding. Weren't you, girls?"

"Yes," from me.

"See, Pat? An accident. A couple of days in bed and Clare will be ready for the wedding with the rest of us."

Auntie Pat shot her a strange, doomed look and huddled deeper within herself.

I tensed and shifted uneasily on my sticky, cracked orange plastic chair, tipping the uneven legs forward for what seemed the millionth time since we'd arrived. After the harrowing ride in the ambulance, I found the slow inefficiency of the hospital almost as frustrating as Auntie Pat did. When at last Uncle Niall approached from the opposite end of the corridor, absorbed in consultation with another doctor, I leapt to my feet along with her.

"Niall—is she going to be all right?" Auntie Pat reached out and clung to Uncle Niall's arm. "Is she?"

Uncle Niall gently removed Auntie Pat from his sleeve. "Shall we go into my office?"

Auntie Faye gestured for Wendy and me to stay where

we were before she helped to lead Auntie Pat off to the staff rooms.

Wendy bent over her magazine when they were gone, avoiding my eyes as I sat down again. We had not been alone since the so-called accident and then I had not stayed with her for long. I had run to Auntie Pat, scraping my knees and bruising my hands in my haste to pull my way out of the maelstrom. True to Clare, I had not told her mother more than the obvious facts and even that edited version had sent her to hysterics and Auntie Faye.

I had my own reasons for keeping quiet. I could not bring myself to repeat the things Wendy had said about Ravenna. They were cruel and seemed directed at me somehow, though their exact intention escaped me. But the very act of remembering, let alone analyzing, turned me to jelly and I must have fitfully dozed off because the next thing I knew Auntie Faye had placed a damp cloth on my forehead.

"Thank goodness you're awake," she said when I opened my eyes. "There's no need for us to be here and I didn't want to burden your uncle with another invalid."

I took another cloth from her and spread it over my hot face at the same time I noticed the room was empty. "Has Clare gone home?"

"Not yet," said Auntie Faye. "I'll explain in the car."

Auntie Faye hurried me outside and into the car. She waited until we were well into the suburbs before she brought up the subject of Clare. "She has had a severe shock and she may not be able to walk for some time. Your Uncle Niall feels it best if she is kept sedated and in the hospital for a while."

My scalp crawled at the words "not able to walk." In an attempt to match Auntie Faye's calm, I asked, "Will she still be in Ravenna's wedding?"

"I'm afraid not. What a fiasco. We're going to have to cancel an usher at this rate. Poor Ravenna. Four attendants looks like we're bargain hunting. It's not what Alan's people would do, I'm sure."

I felt any attendants looked downright inhuman when the youngest member of the wedding was sedated in the hospital. But I knew Auntie Faye too well by now to expect any noble gestures; a postponement might have prevented Ravenna from ever fitting again into Alan Trask's busy appointment calendar.

Back at the house, Ravenna received the news of her cousin's possible paralysis with a distracted "Oh?" before she returned to her more immediate problems. Perhaps it was that she had just opened two identical rice steamers and hadn't a clue what to do with the second one that she accepted the matter so lightly. "Will she be better by the wedding?" she asked, still stumped by the twin appliances.

"I don't think so," said Auntie Faye. She freed Ravenna from the unnecessary second gift and expertly began to re-wrap it for return shipment and exchange. "She's in a bad way. But there's still plenty of time to make alternate arrangements. And I did have a nice thought in the car coming home. We could include a little prayer in the service for her speedy recovery."

Ravenna frowned. "I never heard of a wedding with prayers for the sick," she said.

"But Auntie Pat would appreciate it," Auntie Faye replied. She cut a length of sticky tape. "You always were the one to champion her cause in the past." She turned to me when it was apparent I was hearing more than she liked.

"Have you written up those cards to help the ushers with the seating charts?" she asked pointedly.

I had, but I wanted to be alone. I said I needed another hour or two.

"Well, don't laze about. Make yourself useful."

That evening I learned Auntie Pat did not appreciate the idea of a nice little prayer at Ravenna's wedding. The truth was she didn't seem to appreciate anything to do with Ravenna's wedding anymore and she came around to let everyone know precisely how she felt.

"You can't steam ahead and say a prayer to make it all better!" she wailed, angry and dejected at the same time. "My daughter will never walk again and you speak as though she's no more important than a missing basket of peppermints from the reception!"

"Pat, you must believe I am sorry, no, I'm more than sorry, I'm absolutely horrified at what has happened to Clare," said Auntie Faye when Uncle Niall could do nothing with Auntie Pat's temper. "But don't exaggerate. Don't say she will never walk again. It's negative and you'll upset

Ravenna. She's out with Alan tonight and I don't want her to hear a whisper of this visit."

Auntie Pat snorted. "You have always been insensitive, Faye. I don't know why I expected you to change for the sake of a little girl."

"Clare wouldn't want any changes," Auntie Faye argued, impervious to any slings or slights on her sensitivity. "She was looking forward to the wedding. Think how terrible she would feel if she ever found out she had caused a disruption of some sort.

"Don't you agree, Niall?"

"Definitely. Keep the child happy by all means."

"Clare will be fine," Auntie Faye concluded. "Besides, it isn't in our nature to stop. We didn't stop for Vida. We carried on. And she was dead."

Auntie Pat began to cry. "I just want to know why they were on that blasted hillside in the first place," she said, finally mowed down by Auntie Faye's bulldozer theory of life. A late summer shower joined her tears like a sympathetic Greek chorus, and I left the room before she recovered enough to ask any further, awkward questions.

I was permitted to visit Clare with Ravenna the day before the wedding. Still without feeling in her legs, Clare was drowsy and unsociable from the heavy doses of medication she was spoon-fed on the hour. Even Ravenna's attempts to make her upcoming ceremony sound more than routine failed to rouse her and her eyes remained sleepily focused on the dress she was to have worn the next day. Ironed and wrapped in cellophane, it hung on the back of her door where Auntie Pat had placed it like an icon of baby pink hope.

After a few minutes we quickly ran out of things to say and we anxiously agreed with the nurse who came in to tell us Clare was tiring and we needed to leave.

But once we were outside the private room courtesy of Uncle Niall, Ravenna's mood turned hard as steel. "How did she fall?"

I stood on one leg, scratching the back of it with my other foot. "I don't know. She just did. Let's go."

"Not until you explain what happened."

I looked into those silver eyes. "You're reading too much into this. Maybe you've got those pre-wedding nerves the magazines are always writing about."

"I do not!" Ravenna blushed and lowered her voice. "I just want to know what happened."

For days I had wanted to rid myself of the memory. Knowing I was probably saying it all wrong, but incapable of a polite version with her glowering at me, I let the basics tumble out: "Wendy said you were in a hurry to marry Alan Trask because you were pregnant and Clare tried to defend you and Wendy got angry and pushed her." Behind us I could hear the clatter of nurses delivering afternoon tea on their metal carts and I had the feeling it was high time we were gone.

Dazed, Ravenna was unaware of her surroundings. "I never thought people would see a short engagement like that," she said slowly, sounding worried. "Who else thinks it's true?"

"Nobody." I felt a surge of remorse for telling; she had so patently missed the point. "Look," I said, feeling nervous, "just forget it. Clare doesn't want to blame Wendy for some bizarre reason. She doesn't want us to tell anyone."

"But I have to tell Mummy," Ravenna said. "She has to know it isn't true."

"It is true. Wendy did push Clare. She just let her fall—it was horrible."

"Oh, that doesn't matter now," Ravenna fretted. "Clare fell and the damage is done. But if people are talking about me behind my back...." She shook her head.

I was shocked. "You don't think it matters Wendy shoved Clare over a cliff?"

Flustered, Ravenna started to walk down the hallway. "That's for Wendy and Clare to deal with, not us. Not when everyone in town is gossiping about me."

"It's not people. It's Wendy."

"Wendy had to hear it from someone. She wouldn't have made it up. She's my bridesmaid!" Blindly, Ravenna headed outside to the taxi stand, leaving me to chase after. "I have to tell Mummy," she insisted when I caught up.

The moment we were dropped off at the house, she flew into the kitchen where Auntie Faye was adding the final touches to Ravenna's favorite, and last unmarried, casserole. Without any reference to Wendy or Clare, Ravenna removed the carefully grated cheese sprinkled over a bed of green beans, mushrooms, and tiny pearl onions while she poured out her grievances to her mother. As she listened, Auntie Faye stood very still, her paring knife poised in the air as if ready to slice all gossipmongers to mincemeat. Yet as soon as Ravenna was finished, she returned unruffled to peeling her carrots and dicing her cabbage heads.

"People are envious," she said, glancing at the pile of cheese. "Don't pay them any mind."

"I have to. It's a terrible thing to say. What if Alan hears?"

"He won't. Now why don't you go lie down for an hour or so and when you get up we'll have a cup of tea before supper."

Meekly, Ravenna let her mother take charge. She suddenly looked exhausted, which was odd as it was me and Auntie Faye doing all the work and thinking these days. Ravenna's only required participation was to let herself be moved from one pre-wedding party to the next like an exquisite, breakable doll that was now badly in need of rewinding.

Auntie Faye's crisp voice splintered my thoughts. "How is Clare getting on?" she asked.

"The same."

"Good." She looked at me over a pile of vegetable peelings. "As long as she remains stable we know where we are. And we have to get through this wedding. Then we can think about Clare. We'll make it up to her later, but first Ravenna must be safely married." She smiled.

"Why don't you check the place cards?" she added, as though nothing unusual had occurred. But she called me back as I went to leave. "This nonsense about the rumors," she said. "Forget it, won't you?"

I didn't know how to reply. The smallest details, from the red bottlebrush flowers dropping from the *pohutakawa* trees to the holes in Clare's socks were impossible to forget. Instead, I took my place card list from others of its kind and went to the lounge where I could examine my feelings in private.

A light drizzle covered the sun and brought in a smell of freshly dug soil. I studied the names on my list, stopping when I saw scribbled at the end in Auntie Faye's most cryptic hand, Uncle Morgan and Auntie Sheena. More surprisingly, their names were followed by those of my cousins, Rory and Andrew. I had not seen or heard from their side of the family in over a year. The invitation to the farm had never, as far as I knew, materialized. More likely, I thought as I tried to remember what my boy cousins had been like, it had been stopped by Auntie Faye.

"When did Uncle Morgan decide to come?" I asked her when she came in to see if I was finished with the cards.

"He didn't. It was Sheena's decision. She rang up out of the blue and said she thought they could manage it, seeing they're bringing Rory up to the university this weekend."

"Rory's going to the university?"

"Mmm. Fancy, they're allowing him to go to the art school. I can scarcely believe my brother could be so wasteful. Or frivolous," she said righteously. She sat across from me and began to go through the cards herself.

Just as Auntie Faye reached the end, Ravenna came into the room with an undisguised pout and flopped down beside her mother. "Scarcely believe what?"

"Your cousin, Rory. Don't concern yourself over him of all people. Tomorrow's the big day. You want to be rested. It's a good thing Alan chose to skip all the hooey of a rehearsal. If he's got people from Argentina visiting his refrigeration plant, his business needs to come first and sleep is what you need most."

Ravenna groaned and stretched her legs. "I've never been so tired in my life," she complained.

"You should have stayed in bed longer." The oven timer buzzed and Auntie Faye stood up. "Have you made sure the hairdresser can meet us at the church in the morning?"

"Yes, Mummy. She said she'd be early."

Auntie Faye grunted her approval and left the room.

"You didn't tell her about Wendy," I said, uncertain whether I should be glad or sorry.

"I told her what Wendy said. Isn't that bad enough?" She pushed back her cuticles with her thumbnail. "Anyway, if you're so concerned, why don't you tell her?" She glanced up at me from under her lashes when I didn't reply. "It feels like a dream, doesn't it? One of those weird ones you can't wake up from and yet you have to believe it will end all right. If you don't, it gets worse and worse."

"So what will happen when we wake up?"

Ravenna laughed. "Clare will be fine, Alan and I will have five children and be deliriously happy, and you'll be running the whole show at Whitworth's with a huge salary and lots of successful clients."

I shuddered. "My part sounds like a nightmare."

"That is entirely a matter of opinion."

"Don't you want to get married?" For one crazed moment I thought there was still time for Ravenna to make a dash for freedom.

Ravenna looked at me as if I had lost my mind. "What a thing to say! Of course I want to get married. Besides, even if I didn't, you can't just stop these things. The very idea is horrible. The talk, the gossip, and on top of all this other scandal…."

"For the hundredth time, there is no scandal. Wendy was simply being hateful."

"By repeating what she's heard." She rubbed her temples, hard. "What if everyone starts talking and whispering as I walk down the aisle?"

Auntie Faye returned from the kitchen, still clutching her knife. "If you're talking about Wendy and those rumors again I will be more than upset with both of you."

"We're talking about place settings," Ravenna said from behind closed eyes. "Flowers, water glasses, soup spoons."

Auntie Faye didn't look convinced. "All of that is under control. Now cheer up and come and tell me if this salad dressing is right. I want your last night home with us to be perfect. Come on."

Whatever Auntie Faye said to Ravenna when they were alone in the kitchen must have worked because Ravenna's spirits improved throughout the evening and well past dinner, reminding me of her earlier, carefree self, the one I thought I knew. The night spent as a family *was* perfect, even if the weather didn't agree.

It rained all that night and into the next morning, which wasn't the way Auntie Faye or the photographer had planned it. Cold, icy rain beat the roof until Auntie Faye had to yell in order to be heard over the din.

"Ravenna, try and eat some toast!

"Your suit is on the bed, Niall! The bed!

"Stop moping, Elizabeth! It's a wedding, for heaven's sake."

Caught between the rain and Auntie Faye, I had a mild understanding of aerial warfare.

Auntie Pat and Wendy arrived while we were still racing around in our dressing gowns. Puffed from their sprint up the drive, they tracked in the perpetual mud Auntie Faye was for once too preoccupied to see.

"I apologize for being in a state of undress," Uncle Niall said in as dignified a manner as he could when they discovered him eating scrambled eggs in his pajamas.

"Well, we're not ready yet, either," Auntie Pat said. She shook rainwater onto the floor from her tartan raincoat. "Brian's spending the morning up at the hospital with Clare. He'll meet us at the church."

"He better not be late," Auntie Faye said, her gaze set

firmly on Ravenna.

We were to dress at the church and Auntie Faye lost no time organizing us with suitcases and makeup kits and into the cars. When we arrived we were early enough to find the hairdresser and the men from the flower shop milling around in the gloom, busy decorating the aisles with the last of the garlands and setting out foil pie plates to catch the leaks from the roof. Roses and frangipani blended with the smell of mildewed hymnals in a sweet, unhealthy scent; while the ping-ping of the rain hitting the pie plates followed us all the way back to the vestry.

As soon as we closed the door behind us we got down to business: Ravenna submitted zombie-like to the attention of the hairdresser; Wendy and I slipped into pink chiffon without exchanging a single word; Aunties Faye and Pat battled with boned and fortified lavender suits as though dressing for an execution. The cramped atmosphere was as heavy as the weather.

A momentary respite from each from other came when Mattie Grateful and her mother-in-law, Dot, peeked in on us, each with a large rectangular box. "We brought our pressies with us," Mattie said. "Sorry we didn't drop them off at the house earlier."

"Just put them down anywhere," Auntie Faye directed with a sniff as she hooked up the back of Ravenna's dress. Mattie was sufficiently tickled with the results of her sewing to ignore Auntie Faye's incivility.

"Stunning, if I say so myself," she declared.

It was my first privileged glimpse of Ravenna's wedding dress and it was so beautiful it gave me chills. Solid white lace with a low waist and long sleeves; to be worn just the once seemed tragic.

Ravenna was as stupefied by the loveliness of her gown as the rest of us. As if overcome by a good fortune she could not fathom the meaning of, she let her starched skirts and the stiff cage of the bodice hold her upright while Mattie arranged the patterned veil over her face.

When Auntie Faye was satisfied Ravenna needed no improvement, she made a little show of giving Wendy and me our gifts for being bridesmaids: silver hearts on sterling silver chains Dot Grateful said must have cost a packet. The date together with Alan and Ravenna's initials was engraved on the back of each heart. Expensive or not, around my neck the heart suddenly felt like granite, and Wendy couldn't even be bothered to undo her clasp. I put my hand over the chain to warm it when the first pendulous peals of music strained through the door.

"Oh, there's the organ!" Mattie squealed, hesitant to leave her creation to the care of mere mortals. "Dotsie and I should go out front now," she added. "You've no idea what a crowd there is."

She sent Ravenna an air kiss. "Good luck, sweetie. You look like an angel gone to heaven."

Dot giggled in approval of her daughter-in-law's skills and sentiment. As she turned to go, her heavy lime tent dress almost knocked over Uncle Niall when he came in at last, holding out his hands as if scrubbed for surgery.

Auntie Faye gave Ravenna a wistful, controlled hug and said to us all, "Now you girls remember how to walk? Nice and slow. Keep repeating it to yourselves: nice—and—slow." She backed out of the room at the required pace, then turned and left with a suppressed sob.

We waited until she was quite gone and Uncle Niall had taken Ravenna's arm through his own before Wendy and I followed them out the door.

It's not like a wedding at all, I thought as Mendelssohn's chords rolled out to greet us like a dirge. Gray stone skies and sodden earth, it was like finally attending my mother's funeral.

Chapter Nine

F aithful to the dates stated on her travel brochures, Ravenna came back from a two-week honeymoon in Fiji at six o'clock on a Sunday night, an event reported in Monday's papers. But to Auntie Faye's utter chagrin, Ravenna did not personally inform us of her arrival for another five days.

During that awkward interval, I played second best while Auntie Faye disguised her emotions by having Ravenna's wedding dress dry-cleaned and hermetically sealed in plastic. She then hung the dress in her own closet and with a great deal of badly camouflaged vexation, waited to be summoned to Ravenna's new home.

The house itself was another source of annoyance to Auntie Faye. Purchased by Alan Trask several years prior to his marriage, he had never actually lived in it. Nonetheless he was painstaking about maintenance. He was also very particular concerning security. No matter how hard she cajoled or conspired, he would not give Auntie Faye a key.

"The decorators will take care of everything, Mrs. St. James," he told her at the reception over sparkling wine and crayfish in cream sauce. "There is no need to involve yourself."

"Surely there is some small thing I can do while you're gone, to save expense."

"There is no need, Mrs. St. James."

Yet our fears of permanent exile were soon put to rest. Ravenna rang on a Friday afternoon and in a fit of wifely domesticity, asked us to tea within the hour.

"You can wear one of your Whitworth's outfits," Auntie Faye suggested when she realized I was still in my holiday shorts. She put down the phone. "Appearances matter in the city. It's different over there." She spoke as if Ravenna had gone to live on Mars rather than a painless drive away; a drive she had memorized from studying maps for the past several weeks.

When we finally pulled up outside the three-storied brick and stuccoed house commanding a view of the entire street and beyond, Auntie Faye waited a minute to collect her thoughts while she checked the door locks. The street was muffled in silence. With autumn approaching, the air was thick with the smell of smoke and wet leaves, giving me a moment's uncertainty when Auntie Faye staunchly marched forward and rang the bell.

Out of breath and swathed in a robe of colorful Indian cottons, Ravenna seemed her old self, smiling and greeting us with a hundred unrelated topics at once. "Where have you been? I've been waiting ages! Come on, come in," she said, hugging her mother, hugging me, and ushering us both into a spacious tiled entry hall.

"Here's your dress, dear." Auntie Faye handed over the bag she had remembered to bring with us.

Ravenna laughed, a high-pitched trill of sheer excitement, and she tossed the wedding dress over the stair rails before she went on to show us what she called "the most magnificent house she had ever seen."

I took in the Afghan carpets and samurai swords attached to the *kauri* paneling. Life-sized oil paintings; marble and glass tables; pottery urns taller than my arms could measure: "It's like living in a museum," I exclaimed. "How did Alan find all these things?"

Auntie Faye retrieved the dress bag from the staircase. "The decorators, I suppose," she said. She held up the bag and shook out the creases.

Ravenna laughed again. "Mummy, leave that. There's still so much I have to show you." Auntie Faye's face fell, but she dutifully followed as Ravenna led us to a sitting room at the very back of the house that faced a terraced rose garden. The combination of late roses, artfully weathered flagstones, and terracotta statuary did a great deal to revive Auntie Faye's spirits.

"What a lovely oasis," she said. She sank almost against her will into a Florentine tooled leather couch. "What's Alan doing?"

"Working, of course. But we don't need him, do we? I've got heaps you haven't seen yet and I've made coffee. I'm afraid I couldn't find any tea."

"Shall I bring it in?" Auntie Faye stood in search of the kitchen.

"No, no. Sit down," Ravenna ordered. "I've got it all ready. Won't be a sec." She scampered away through a side door, leaving a confused impression of printed skirts and musky perfume. Despite its luxury, the room without her seemed absolutely lifeless.

"Marriage agrees with her," Auntie Faye whispered to me in a voice signifying she had known this would happen. She then became too absorbed in the marvel of Alan's taste and bank account to say anything further.

Ravenna came back gasping then smiling at her ineptitude as she almost dropped an entire coffee set at our feet. "Sorry." She juggled the milk and sugar before she gave up and left them on the tray.

I went to help her. "I'm still getting used to things here," she apologized. "The kitchen is far too big for me. So many cupboards and they open so fast on these fancy European hinges. They just swing out at you! I've got an enormous bump on my head. Fortunately, Alan's hired a girl to come and look after me three days a week." She finally got the order right for pouring the coffee and she handed me a cup with the seriousness of a child playing mothers and fathers with twigs and stones.

"These cups are nice," I said to cover the sudden silence.

"They're awfully modern," Auntie Faye countered. She lifted an angular pitcher to the light with a twinge of her usual disapproval of anything that wasn't Royal Doulton,

Wedgwood, or Worcester.

"Surely you haven't forgotten this set," Ravenna said. She sliced several pieces of cake. "The girls at the hospital gave it to me. Alan doesn't like it either."

Auntie Faye set the pitcher down. "I can see why." She watched Ravenna's bungled efforts with the knife, and then asked, "Is that wedding cake?"

"Mm-hm. I saved the top layer for our first anniversary like the magazines said to do and then there was all this left. Don't you want any?"

"It's just a bit depressing. I don't like to be reminded we haven't got you to ourselves any longer."

Ravenna balanced the remaining cups and saucers in a stack she set aside with difficulty. "You have Elizabeth," she pointed out.

Auntie Faye reached for the top cup and put it straight. "Yes," she said inconclusively. "We have Elizabeth." She waited for Ravenna to sit before she asked, "Who's this girl you've got coming in?"

"Someone from the university. Alan says they're the best because they do want the job, usually appreciate nice things, and you don't have to pay them very much." Ravenna sipped her coffee before she made a face at the bitterness. "I guess Rory's up at the university now," she added. "Did you see him at my reception, Elizabeth?"

"For a minute." I had had only the briefest glimpse of that entire branch of the family at the reception. Auntie Faye had been determined to get her money's worth out of me for those silver chains, and I had spent most of my time serving drinks and clearing tables.

"He's become much nicer than before. More grown-up," Ravenna mused.

Auntie Faye pursed her lips. "His suit was too tight."

"Artists don't need suits," I said.

Auntie Faye left the last of her coffee. "May we see the rest of the house now, dear?"

Ravenna seemed relieved to drop the unwanted subject of Rory and soon we were off on a tour of pantries, bedrooms, libraries—his and hers—and a combination bar and billiards room. Obviously staggered by the amount of property her marriage had brought, Ravenna saved what she considered the best for last with a flourish.

"You will not believe this," she said, drawing us through her white and ivory bedroom. Before Auntie Faye could exclaim over the fineness of the linens or the extent of the thick sheepskin rugs, Ravenna pushed open a mirrored door. "Look," she commanded. The open door revealed a coral pink and cut-glass bathroom, a most inadequate term for something straight out of the Roman Empire.

Auntie Faye put a hand to her throat. "Never in my wildest dreams...." She bent down and gently stroked the gold faucets.

Ravenna giggled. "Go on, try them."

Warily, Auntie Faye pulled on the tail of a gilt dolphin and watched the water gush out of its open mouth. After a minute she turned the water off and stood frozen in the face of such extravagance. "You are very lucky, Ravenna," she said in a voice edging toward somber. "This is all much, much more than I expected. It almost frightens me."

Ravenna shivered, rippling the deep flounces on her dress. "Don't talk like that, Mummy. You're scaring me now and I'm the one who has to live here." She turned to me. "So when are you coming to stay?"

I wanted to say, "Why even go home?" but Auntie Faye put her arm protectively around Ravenna as they started together back down the stairs. "I'm afraid you and Elizabeth will both be too busy for idle visits," she said. "Elizabeth will be back at Whitworth's next week and you have to start making social contacts. They will be the most important contribution you can make to Alan's business interests. You certainly have the room and facilities for some first-class entertaining."

"But if that's true, then wouldn't it be good for Elizabeth to meet people here?"

"Studying hard will be even better. Elizabeth has to be practical. She understands."

I was beginning to understand less and less, but I also knew Auntie Faye thought Ravenna was being naive. My irregular background was not a desirable trait for entry into the best families, the same families it was now Ravenna's duty to charm and entertain. I would never catch an Alan Trask, even if I wanted to, which I certainly did not, but my destiny as Auntie Faye saw it was to fend for myself in the world of industry and commerce.

When we were downstairs, Auntie Faye excused herself to go in search of more dolphins, and Ravenna began turning the remaining cake into little parcels she pressed me to take.

"What am I going to do with cake?" I asked. I didn't think I could bear to look at another slice of the rich stuff.

"What about Wendy and Clare? Give it to them."

I looked into Ravenna's eyes, noting with perplexity the over-bright sparkle, and said, "They couldn't possibly want it. Clare is barely conscious and Wendy hasn't spoken to me for a month."

Ravenna smoothed down her skirt and then fluffed it up again to watch the printed fabric billow and fall. "I meant what I said upstairs about having you come to stay," she said. "Just give me some time. Everything will work out, you'll see."

Auntie Faye rejoined us, searching through her handbag for her car keys as she did so. "What's that, Ravenna?"

"Nothing, Mummy. Are you going straight home from here?"

Auntie Faye found the keys and snapped her bag shut. "I thought we'd call on Clare first and see if your father needs anything. We really have to go now or we'll miss visiting hours. Give our love to Alan, won't you? When do you expect him back?"

"Soon. We're going to some people's house for dinner."

"Business associates?"

"Probably. I don't think Alan has many of what you

could call actual friends."

Auntie Faye handed me my cardigan. "Make a good impression and be sure to get their address so you can write and thank them for their hospitality. We should also start planning a reciprocal dinner for them in return, just to be prepared for when it best suits Alan's diary."

"Yes, Mummy."

Not quite out the door, Auntie Faye turned. "Don't forget to hang up your wedding dress before it wrinkles."

"No, Mummy."

Ravenna stood in the wide, double doorway to see us off; a kind of frantic desperation in her farewell. But that must have only been the way I saw it, because the first thing Auntie Faye said when we were inside the car was, "Ravenna has never looked happier. I knew this move was right."

"I thought she seemed funny."

"Funny?" Auntie Faye turned the wheel. "Why are you trying to tarnish things? Don't you want her to be happy?"

"Yes, of course, but—"

"But nothing," Auntie Faye concluded. "Anyway," she said, "you're far too young to understand these things."

Twenty minutes later we were at the hospital for a final visit with Clare. Having been pronounced incurable, she was going home the next day.

Auntie Pat sat stationed by her daughter's bedside with her knitting needles and a skein of red wool on her lap when we entered the room on tiptoe. "Booties," she explained. She held up the shapeless bundle for our inspection. "The circulation in her feet is getting bad."

Auntie Faye would not be swayed from her mission of joy by talk of poor circulation. She was so inflated from her recent success with Ravenna she was able to sail to Clare's shrunken side on pure good will. "Wake up, dear," she said, hovering over her niece's pinched, yellow face. "Wake up and look at me."

Clare remained motionless and Auntie Pat let out a long breath as she scraped her knitting needles together. "I did think Clare would fight more," she said. "I've tried to kindle a response in her," she added with a nod toward the brides-maid dress still on its hanger and now collecting dust, "but it's no use."

As though she had been listening to every word, Clare gritted her teeth and shifted beneath the heavy blanket. Immediately, her mother left her knitting and moved closer to the bed. "There, there," she crooned.

Clare made a sort of mewing noise and Auntie Pat said, "Look, chookie. Who's come to see you, then?"

Restlessly, Clare opened her eyes for a moment before she slid back into a newly remembered babyhood and shut them again.

"I'm sorry," Auntie Pat said to us as she stroked and cuddled Clare further into oblivion.

Auntie Faye dragged a chair across the floor and sat down. She indicated I should do the same. "Not to worry," she said. "Clare will improve once you get her home."

"Going home terrifies me, Faye. I don't know how we

will manage. I feel so alone."

"You'll have the public health nurse. And the physical therapist. Every day if you like, Niall says. You will hardly be alone."

Satisfied that Clare had gone back to sleep, Auntie Pat returned to her knitting and said, "Sheena is coming by later. I hope she won't be hurt if Clare doesn't react."

"Sheena's still in town?" Auntie Faye sat up straighter. "Why hasn't anyone told me? Where's Morgan?" She looked at me as if being left out of the loop were somehow my fault.

Auntie Pat switched to smaller needles. "Morgan had to go back down to the farm after Ravenna's reception, but with Rory enrolling at the university, Sheena wanted to do some shopping and make sure he was settled."

"Sounds like coddling to me," said Auntie Faye. She watched her sister's fingers labor through a purl row and then suddenly stop.

"Oh, Faye," she said, the unfinished bootie in her lap. "I am so embarrassed. I quite forgot to thank you."

Auntie Faye narrowed her eyes. "Thank me for what?"

"Wendy's job."

"What job?"

"With Alan."

Auntie Faye leaned closer as if visibly sniffing trouble. "I have no idea what you're talking about," she said coldly.

"Alan Trask has offered Wendy a job. I thought you were behind it all. I mean, you usually are."

Auntie Faye ignored this last remark. "We were at Ravenna's a few minutes ago and she never said a word." She looked across at me. "Did she say anything to you?" I shook my head. "Oh, this is becoming very tiresome. I'm beginning to believe nobody pays me any mind whatsoever."

Auntie Pat studied the front of her knitting pattern. "Perhaps Ravenna doesn't know anything about it yet. She's only been back from her honeymoon a few days, hasn't she? Anyway, it was such an opportunity for Wendy. Two hours each day after school and her weekends free. We are very, very pleased."

Auntie Faye couldn't contain her frustration any longer. "But this is ridiculous," she burst out. "Wendy has no experience, no training. It's Elizabeth we're spending a fortune on to send to Whitworth's Business Academy! If anyone needs a job, it's Elizabeth. She and Ravenna are as close as sisters!"

"Elizabeth is too young," Auntie Pat protested. "Wendy is a bit older, after all." She turned her head to me. "You don't feel slighted, do you, Elizabeth?"

"No—"

Auntie Faye cut me off. "We must be going," she said in a last ditch effort to remain in control of the situation. "Ravenna is holding her first dinner party in a few weeks and I want to start pricing things for her."

Busy with her tangled handiwork, Auntie Pat did not seem over-concerned to see us go and we left on a sharp note of aggravation.

"Alan was simply being kind," Auntie Faye rationalized as we walked into the empty corridor. "Probably because of all this trouble with Clare, who has become in my opinion, frightfully difficult. Especially when Niall says it's all in her mind."

"I don't understand." The afternoon was going from bad to worse.

"This play-acting about not moving her legs. It's a hysterical reaction, though to what, who knows."

I looked down at the floor and Auntie Faye said, "I have to find your uncle. Don't you dare wander off." She hurried away, leaving me rooted to the spot. The second she was gone I saw Auntie Sheena approach with her two sons, the infamous Rory and the less rebellious Andrew.

"Elizabeth," she said warmly. "How nice to see you here. We barely had time to see you at the reception; Faye had you working so hard. How are you, dear?"

"Auntie Faye had to go find Uncle Niall," I said, in a sudden panic to find myself without her bulwark. I had no idea what to say with two teenage boys, one of them reported to be artistic and dangerous, so close.

Auntie Sheena laughed at my confusion. "Did you visit Clare?" she asked.

"Clare's asleep."

Auntie Sheena seemed disconcerted by the news. "Oh. Well, I'll just peek in for a moment. Coming, boys?"

Andrew opened the door for his mother, but Rory held back. "I can't stand illness," he said. "I told you I wasn't going in."

His brother waited; his hand on the door while their mother hesitated. "I don't want to insist," she said.

"Then don't, Mum. Please."

Auntie Sheena smiled. "Don't go away," she said. She stepped into Clare's room with Andrew.

Rory shook his head when they were gone. "Bloody miserable place, this," he said, a curl to his lip.

I remained silent and he crossed his arms over his paint-splattered T-shirt and inclined his head toward the door. "You must think I'm a hard case not wanting to go in there," he said, "but I'm put off by sickness and imperfection. The whole medical scene disgusts me."

"It's not Clare's fault."

Rory shrugged and produced a tobacco tin and a packet of cigarette papers from his pockets. "She should have been more careful."

"She was." I watched him choose a paper and a plug of tobacco. "She was careful," I repeated.

"What's that supposed to mean?"

"Wendy pushed her." The words were out of my mouth before I could stop them.

"How interesting. Who else knows?"

I looked at his scruffy clothes and uncut hair and saw a core of energy that set him apart from the Haddon clan in a way I found myself admiring. "I told Ravenna."

"Ravenna the sacrificial lamb," he said more to himself than to me as he rolled his cigarette. "So it's three of us sharing a little secret. Very droll. Although I must confess, I could never abide Wendy or even Ravenna for that matter." He took a lighter from his other pocket.

I turned when I heard the stamp of Auntie Faye's sensible shoes bearing down on the linoleum. She took one look at Rory's unlit cigarette. "Excuse me," she said, pointing to a large red sign on the opposite wall. "I believe this says, 'No Smoking.'" Rory didn't reply and Auntie Faye asked, "Where's your mother?"

"Inside doing her good deed for the day."

"Why aren't you?"

Rory regarded her with a long, cool look Auntie Faye gave him right back. "Come along, Elizabeth," she finally said in the same tone she'd been directing me about with all day. "We must be off." Without waiting to see Auntie Sheena, she rushed me outside to the car park.

Dark clouds scudded across the sun, giving me the same uneasy feeling I had talking to Rory. "What a business," she said at last.

"About Clare?"

"Clare and Wendy and everything else," Auntie Faye said, walking faster. "That Rory strikes me as extremely bad-mannered. I'm sure the university will make him worse than ever. Art school," she pronounced as if the very words had a taste beyond vile.

"Why does everyone think art school is so terrible?" I asked, running to catch up with her.

Auntie Faye stopped in the middle of the footpath and

regarded me carefully. "Because it does nothing but encourage lazy people like your cousin Rory to think the world of themselves and scrounge off society for the rest of their lives. You shouldn't even need to ask."

"But it can't be like that for everyone. I think it sounds fun."

"Is this a hint?"

"No, I'm just saying art school might be more fun than typing, that's all."

"Are you unhappy at Whitworth's?" Auntie Faye looked at me as if she were to hear one more wrong answer she would throw us both in front of a bus.

"I don't think you could call it 'unhappy,'" I said, trying to define exactly what it was I felt for the dreary office block that housed the school.

"Think carefully what you would call it," Auntie Faye advised, "because your Uncle Niall wants you to be a success and he would be heartsick if you changed your mind this late in the day."

I didn't think Uncle Niall could care less what I did as long as I stayed out of his way, but the whole idea of having my future mapped out so precisely was beginning to scare me. "What if I change?" I asked, growing more and more worried. "What if I could dance or act or paint, or even got engaged, like Ravenna?"

Auntie Faye straightened her back in a flood of relief and resumed walking as if the proverbial monkey had flown from her shoulders. "You," she said, "aren't Ravenna."

Chapter Ten

No, I was not Ravenna, and never could be. And with each dull, passing day as I waited to resume my classes at Whitworth's Business Academy, the fact became increasingly evident to both myself and Auntie Faye.

Whitworth's, whatever Auntie Faye claimed to be its reputation, was a low-budget concern run by a staff of three and located on the fringe of the commercial district. "But it's grounding you in the basics," Auntie Faye assured me the Monday I started my second year of attendance. "Unlike Wendy and this so-called 'internship' with Alan, you'll be prepared for anything. All she is going to know is how to stock a supermarket shelf. And what's the good of that at the end of the day?"

"She can always go to another supermarket," I said. "People still have to eat."

Auntie Faye folded, and then refolded the top of my lunch bag as she decided whether she agreed with me or merely deplored my attitude. "You'll be late," she finally said.

By the end of the afternoon I wished I could have been expelled as well as late. Deplorably similar to ordinary school, Whitworth's was run along childish rules and regulations. Punctuality reigned supreme; my classmates were clique-ish and moronic; mediocrity was well rewarded. No one took much notice of me and I scraped by somewhere in the middle of the bunch. That didn't prevent Auntie Faye from continuing to supervise my life over the following weeks with a ruthless demand for detail.

"Have you started dictation yet? How many words a minute can you type? Only forty? I hear some of the girls in your class are up to sixty-three." The situation was at times intolerable and I had the impression we were both keeping mental calendars, scoring off the days until I was out the door and self-supporting.

But if Auntie Faye took any consolation in visions of me headed for financial independence, it was tempered by Ravenna, or rather, Ravenna's sudden, and inevitable, self-sufficiency.

During those first few months of her marriage, Ravenna was protected by a barricade of social functions that grew and multiplied to such a degree that we never saw her except as a photo in the newspaper. Many were Auntie Faye's attempts to storm this fortress of activity, but each new coup was destined for failure. The sausage rolls she insisted on baking, unasked, for Ravenna's numerous club meetings and business teas turned cold and rancid several times before she realized they were not wanted. It was Uncle Niall who stopped her.

"We don't fit in," he said one night from over his news-paper. "Don't take it personally, but to Alan and Ravenna and that crowd, we're passé. We're old. They don't want us at their parties. Let it be, Faye, and stop making those confounded rolls. I'm sure Elizabeth's sick to death of taking them in her lunch. I know I am."

"I'm trying to be of some small service," Auntie Faye said, suppressing a good cry as she rinsed off the baking sheets. "And I can't say I'm not offended when I am. It's not natural. A young girl like Ravenna shouldn't be cut off from her mother and made to cope with all those people on her own."

Natural or not, Ravenna did cope and according to the clippings Auntie Faye collected, she coped very well. But despite her regular, weekly phone calls, Ravenna had become a stranger to us, and reading about Mrs. Trask was not the same as being with her.

"I never expected her to turn her back on us," Auntie Faye said more than once.

My escape from Whitworth's and Auntie Faye's grum-bling was to go up to the university during lunchtime. It was within walking distance and if I wasn't allowed a place there, I could mingle and dream. After all, Auntie Faye had been telling me to mingle since the day I got off the boat.

I knew I was out of place at the university, but it seemed to me I was out of place wherever I went. My young age and neutral, polyester-based presence singled me out as an oddity amidst the jeans and basic black, but I didn't care. Those breaks from class when I could wander freely through the bookstore, skimming through texts on everything from medieval architecture to humanistic psychology were risks well worth the taking.

What I hadn't bargained for was meeting up with Rory. Auntie Faye would have kept me home from even Whitworth's if she had known I had seen him from a short distance one day in the quad. He hadn't changed much since I had seen him last, though he did seem more confident and more aware of the effect he had on the people around him clamoring for his attention. The next time I ran into him was at such close proximity I had to speak up regardless of my misgivings.

We were outside the Student Union coffee bar and at first he gave me such a glassy stare I had to remind him who I was: "Elizabeth. Haddon. Your cousin. You probably don't remember."

"But I do. You were at the hospital that day. What are you doing here? Are you a child prodigy or something?"

I shook my head. "I just like it here."

Rory continued to stare until his friends started to voice their impatience. "Hang on," he told them over his shoulder. Turning back to me, he said, "Do you want to go inside?"

The invitation confused me and I said, "I can't. I have to be back at Whitworth's in twenty minutes."

"Come inside for ten," he said. He pushed open the

door and we went to a table. When we were seated next to a concrete wall surrounded by graffiti-covered posters and students of all ages, he said, "You're different from what I remember." The din of multiple conversations required him to shout.

I glanced at my beige twill skirt. "Are you sure you don't mean 'more boring'?"

"Would you model for me?"

"Model for you?" I nearly fell out of my chair. "You have got to be joking. Auntie Faye would kill me. And you."

"What's Auntie Faye got to do with it? I'm serious. It would be a big help to me. You should see the models they provide at the art school. It would be great to work with someone young and underweight for a change. How about this afternoon?"

"You're insane. I can't model this afternoon or ever."

"Why not?"

"Well, for one thing I hardly have the looks to be a model and second, like I said, Auntie Faye would never approve. Never!"

"You could keep your clothes on."

I started to laugh. "Oh, thanks. That will keep Auntie Faye happy."

"She doesn't have to know." Rory began to roll one of the cigarettes that had made Auntie Faye so angry at the hospital. Suddenly everything I was missing out on loomed before me, but I was torn. My lunch hour was up and I was five minutes past the bell. "I have to go," I said. "My typing scores are a disaster."

Rory grabbed my skirt. "Forget about that and stay here. Where's the harm? We are family, after all." He smiled, exactly liked Ravenna when she wanted her own way.

"Let go of my skirt. I'll—scream."

"Go ahead. The odd scream or two would never be heard in this place." Rory waited while I searched for a suitable retort. I couldn't find one, and he said, "Come home with me and forget Dumpworth's or whatever it's called. I haven't any classes this afternoon and I'm going through my dark phase. I need a challenge."

"I can't...."

"Call in sick." He handed me some coins and pointed me in the direction of a wall phone. In a fit of sheer madness I made the call, pleading a headache. Before I could change my mind, we were on the bus.

"You should do something about your clothes," Rory suggested as we lurched from side to side when the bus turned a corner.

"Auntie Faye chooses them. They're meant to be hard-wearing, for business school and after."

"What are you doing at business school, anyway? Isn't that too *bourgeois* and disgusting for words?"

"It's a long story based on economics and family history," I replied. "It's like the clothes: practical." I looked out the bus window and watched the rain stipple the trees.

"Have we much farther to go?"

"Next stop." Rory pulled the bell cord and motioned for me to go with him to the front of the bus.

As soon as we were let out, we turned down a narrow, twisting street lined with shabby Edwardian bungalows and much-neglected flowering shrubs, their heavy branches bent low to the ground. "Is it all students around here?" I asked, walking beside Rory and stepping over the car and bicycle parts littering the footpath.

"Mostly. But at this time of the day they're all up at the library or stuck in lectures. I love coming home when they're gone and the sky is that incredible gray hue. I feel I can get some real work accomplished."

"I would have thought the light was wrong."

"It is, but in this country you get used to things being wrong. I just try to take advantage of what's available and what I can use. Although I assume dear Auntie Faye spins a different tale."

"How did you know?"

"The rumbles of disapproval were so loud I could hear them clear down to Hamilton and beyond even when I was a kid. It was the one subject she and my father actually agreed on."

"Didn't he want you to go to art school either?"

Rory shrugged. "In the beginning he was dead set against it. But Mum talked him round. It helped that Andrew was so keen on the farm. It made it easier to break away.

"I've got my own exhibition in a month," he added,

kicking wet flower petals into the gutter as we walked.

"That's wonderful," I said, although the real wonder to me was the ease with which I found myself able to talk to him.

"Oh, everyone at the school has a show sooner or later," he said. "Mine is just sooner.

"Well, here we are. Start practicing poses." Rory opened a front door peeling paint and missing several panes from a stained glass insert. "My flatmate, Tania, did that," he said, referring to the holes left in the design. "She was making a mobile and desired something blue. Cup of tea?"

"Yes, please." I followed Rory down a hallway that creaked with every step. I did my best to avoid the stacked canvases turned to face the water-damaged gold wallpaper.

"This was a very posh house at one time," Rory said as he guided me past fallen plaster rosettes and more bicycle parts. "It's a bit of a junker now, but it's still got a faded grandeur. Anyway, it's cheap."

"I love it." It was the sort of place I had grown up in when I lived with my mother in London. After nearly two years with Auntie Faye I had almost forgotten the string of haphazard flats and houses I had so gladly turned my back on. Now they seemed almost inviting.

Rory swung open the door to his bedroom studio and onto more of the same chaos. Long tendrils from the vines outside his window pushed their way through cracks in the wall like soft green hands. I went to touch them.

"Sit down. You look frightened," Rory said.

"I'm not frightened, I'm impressed. I've never seen plants growing through the walls." Yet because he wanted me to, I sat down on a ripped silk cushion and breathed in the peculiar smell of bleach, incense, mosquito repellent, and paint thinners while Rory flopped down on a slab of foam rubber.

"Hold your head up higher," he instructed, squinting.

"Why? I haven't agreed to pose for you."

"That's beside the point. Just look out the window and be yourself."

With one hand, Rory felt along the floor and after a moment found a pencil and a scrap of paper. A few seconds later I asked, "How am I meant to get home tonight?"

Rory sighed and flipped the unfinished sketch to the other side. "You shouldn't have moved."

"I couldn't help it. I feel ridiculous." I was beginning to sense the stupidity of missing my afternoon at Whitworth's. Suddenly I wasn't up to inventing excuses for my behavior to Auntie Faye.

"You need to relax," Rory said. "Let's go have that tea."

In the kitchen, Rory talked, mainly about himself. "I couldn't stand to teach when I'm through with the university," he said. "That's what everybody expects me to do, even Mum, but it's a prospect I find nauseating."

"Why should you be a teacher? I mean, after studying to be an artist, why give up one profession for another?"

Rory poured out two mugs of unusually dark tea and said, "You're the first member of this idiot family to call what I'm doing 'a profession.' That's a miracle when you reckon how influenced you must be by Auntie Faye and Ravenna every day of your life."

"Ravenna isn't part of my life these days," I said before blowing across my tea to cool it. A whiff of smoky clay rose from my cup, like damp tree roots or the musty tins of Chinese spices they sold in the decaying shops behind Whitworth's. The steam hung in the air for an isolated second and then evaporated as tracelessly as my friendship with Ravenna had.

Rory studied me for a moment. "What happened with Ravenna?"

"Nothing really. She just drifted away into her marriage. Auntie Faye goes around like the tragic muse about it. 'A daughter's desertion is a hard cross to bear.'" Rory laughed and I said, "I don't think Alan likes us. And he's too busy making money to care that much anyway."

"I hate those business types," Rory said. "I bet he's one of those people with hoards of cash and zilch taste. Right?"

I nodded and his smile turned to a scowl. "The deal is," he said slowly, "is that it's people like Alan Task I will have to depend on if I want to get anywhere with my art. I have to sell to that class because they've got the money and the inclination to cover their walls with something more high-brow than newspaper. It's either that or end up teaching in the local intermediate school and I refuse to compromise. People who compromise are twits."

A noise at the front door made him look up from his tea.

"Tania?" he called out.

"Right the first time," a girl's voice answered from the hallway.

Rory poured more tea. "Tania's the stained glass thief I told you about. You might find her—"

"Find me what?" A tall, attractive part-Maori girl in denim overalls rushed into the room and hit Rory over the head with a sketchbook. "Find me what?"

"Be civilized," Rory chided her. He wrestled the sketchbook away from her and then promptly whacked her on the backside with it. "We've got visitors." He followed his words with a quick hug.

Tania squirmed out of his grasp and helped herself to Rory's tea. She swallowed and gave me a fierce once-over. "I eat visitors," she said.

"Not this one you don't. This is my cousin Elizabeth and she has a difficult life. Leave her alone."

Tania shot me another dagger and asked, "Are you a nurse?"

"No. Do I look like one?"

"Sort of. You're very clean. Prim and proper. Rory doesn't usually bring nice girls home."

Rory took his tea back. "Don't be rude."

Undaunted, Tania sat down and put her feet up on the table. "You haven't asked where I've been today."

"Robbing banks."

"Oh, shut up. Just listen to this and then I'll let you carry on seducing your little nurse. I've got a job."

I cringed at both her words and tone but Rory didn't see me; his attention was fully focused on Tania.

"You?"

"Me. Housecleaning."

Rory let out a laugh. "You're the last person I can see with a broom and mop, taking orders and scrubbing loos."

"Well, it's true. As from next Wednesday I'll be working for Mrs. Alan Trask of Remuera. Quite a trump, eh?"

Rory and I exchanged glances.

"You have heard of Alan Trask, haven't you?" Tania asked.

"Sure," Rory replied. "He's family."

Tania sat up, swinging her feet to the floor. "You never let on you were related to high finance."

"It's not a connection I'm proud of. And there's nothing in it for me. Alan's wife, your new employer, is just another cousin. Elizabeth here lives with her parents."

"Oh." Tania looked at me as if I might be more interesting than the first poor impression I gave. "Perhaps there's a silver lining in this grimy cloud."

"Don't count on it," Rory said. "Elizabeth and I have received nothing from the Trasks except for some stale wedding cake. Awful, wasn't it?" he said as an aside to me. Without waiting for my reply he said to Tania, "We still have to work for a living. Which reminds me." Again he leant my way. "We better get started before the light is completely gone." He pointed me in the direction of his studio.

Tania stood up and went to the sink filled with crusted

plates and burnt skillets. "Is she staying for dinner?"

"Yes," Rory said. I realized I'd be lucky to get back to Auntie Faye before midnight.

Back in Rory's room I returned to my earlier seat on the silk cushion. Rory took up a piece of newsprint and a stick of charcoal and said, "I can't believe Tania's working for Ravenna. I mean, what a day this has been. First you, then Ravenna. I thought I was getting away from my family coming up here."

"Do you mind?"

"No, it's quite enjoyable. I've always taken to women's company. My father and Andrew have limited conversational qualities. Falling wool prices and rolling down to the pub whenever Mum tries her hand at anything more exotic than bangers and mash is about it." Idly, Rory slid behind a large drafting table and began to draw in wide, ungoverned strokes. "Don't move," he commanded although I had remained as still as I could.

A wind blew in through the window and stirred the vines that tumbled over the sill. It was easy to do as Rory asked. Easy to sit still and stop thinking about Whitworth's and Auntie Faye. For a moment I almost understood why Clare had chosen to wrap herself into a warm cocoon of apathy.

Just as I was about to fall asleep, Rory abruptly pushed the sketch away and stood up. "It's no good," he said with a deep stretch. "You'll have to come back."

"What's wrong?"

"Nothing. When you're dreaming like that I could work

all day. But I'd prefer to talk to you."

"To me?"

Rory covered the sketch with a clean piece of paper. "Auntie Faye should be shot," he said matter-of-factly, "because I am getting the distinct impression she has warped your brain."

"Perhaps a little," I agreed.

"Perhaps a lot. And I have decided it is my duty as your eldest male relative to take over. We will start by having dinner, then I will take you home and then maybe in two or three weeks you won't be frightened of me any longer."

"I'm not frightened!"

"Yes, you are. You're terrified. I can see it in your eyes and the way you clutch your middle like that. But I'll make you get used to me. Now come and eat."

The rest of Rory's seven flatmates were in the kitchen when Tania served a dinner of beans over brown rice and roast pumpkin. It was just the sort of meal to send Auntie Faye to bed for a week and I ate every mouthful as if it were my last, figuring it probably would be after Auntie Faye learned where I had been all afternoon.

"You'll be totally corrupted after a few more meals with us," Rory said.

"I don't think that will be for a long time," I replied.

"What about Saturday?" he asked. "I want to show you the gallery where I'm holding my exhibition." Before I could object he went to borrow the keys to a van so he could drive me home.

Later, as we crossed the bridge over the harbor, floodlit in yellow and glistening with rain, he repeated his invitation for Saturday. Trying to keep my voice light, I said, "I don't think Auntie Faye will let me out of the house for at least another year."

"Let me deal with Auntie Faye," he said with more confidence than I possessed.

Auntie Faye wasn't exactly pacing the driveway by the time I got home, but her anger was palpable even from the outside. "Where, where have you been?" she asked, floundering for words. "Your uncle and I were practically crazed with worry. I was nearly on the verge of ringing Ravenna, but she has so much else on her mind right now—"

"You can blame me, Auntie Faye," Rory said. He smiled and ran his hand through his hair. "Elizabeth became unwell this afternoon." And with no account as to how he of all people had managed to come to my supposed rescue, he gave her a story that eventually had her concerned for my health.

"I'm all right now," I murmured, astounded by the effortless way he handled her. "And I did ring Whitworth's."

Rory crossed his arms. "What I wanted to know, Auntie Faye, was if Elizabeth could come back into town with me on Saturday."

Auntie Faye regarded him with suspicion. "Whatever for?"

"To visit the gallery where I'm having an exhibition. She'd be in the best of hands."

"I don't know about that."

I went to her side. "I've caught up with all my assign-
ments," I said, hoping my industry would somehow con-
vince her I needed time off.

She didn't speak and Rory slapped the car keys against
his thigh with a gesture that made her wince.

"It's settled, then," he said, although no one had settled
anything. "See you Saturday."

As soon as he was gone, Auntie Faye turned to me.
"Oh, Elizabeth, I'm not sure about this. He's so rough, and
you're so much younger than he is. This isn't how we raised
Ravenna."

"But he is family," I pointed out. She looked as if she
wished any other family on earth would come forward and
claim him as their own. I tried to soften her distress by
adding, "You'll never believe what, Auntie Faye, but one of
Rory's flatmates has got a job with Ravenna."

"Doing what?"

"Housecleaning."

More irritated than ever, Auntie Faye buttoned her cardigan to the neck. "I wonder why Ravenna is forever
favoring the rest of the family. It strikes me as absurdly
extravagant of her to keep giving her relations jobs."

"Like who?"

"Wendy for one, and now this girl we know nothing
about."

"Tania is only Rory's flatmate and Wendy works for
Alan, not Ravenna."

Auntie Faye pointed me inside to the lounge and drew the curtains shut. When the last sliver of night had been extinguished she took up a brass-framed photo of Ravenna outside the church on her wedding day.

"Lovely, wasn't she?"

I looked over my aunt's shoulder. Wendy and I were in the background, two pink blobs against wet flax and *ti-tree*.

Yes, Ravenna was lovely. Lovely and regal and better than perfect from her smile to the way she held her bouquet just so, displaying her opals and new wedding ring. What little sun there had been on the day flashed off the gold band with a star.

Ravenna was beautiful, but I was going to the art gallery with Rory. I wanted to pinch myself. I might not have been Ravenna, but I was me. For the first time since I had met her, I was glad we were nothing alike.

Chapter Eleven

"I have an idea," Rory said when we were outside on the grass behind the city art gallery. All day he had been full of ideas, making the time speed by, something I regretted when I knew how late it was and how much difficulty I had gone through persuading Auntie Faye to let me be here in the first place.

"What now?" I asked.

Rory's mouth twitched at the corners. "I think you should move into the city."

"Don't joke," I said as I thought how tempting and utterly impossible the prospect was. "Where would I live? More to the point, how would I live? I'm sixteen and they don't pay you to go to Whitworth's." For all his education, Rory knew very little about real life.

"You could move into the flat with the rest of us. There's so many people no one would even notice you." Rory pulled at the grass. "I'd help you out until you got on your feet."

"I thought students were meant to be poor."

Rory laughed. "I'm one of a lucky minority. I get two

scholarships and Mum is fantastic. Come on, Elizabeth, say you will. It makes sense. You wouldn't have to commute to that Whitworth's place any more, and I can tell you've enjoyed yourself today. You like the things the city offers."

"Liking and having are two separate things," I said. I watched the water in a nearby fountain drop over a series of opposing rectangles and I wished my life could be as direct and forceful as its flow.

"You're too passive," Rory complained. "You don't stand up for what you want."

"Nobody ever asked me what I wanted before."

"I'm asking. Right now. If you could decide for yourself, what would you choose to do?"

I didn't need to think about my answer. "Quit Whitworth's for a start." But the rest? I thought for a minute. "Okay. I'd go back to school and then on to the university. I'm not sure what I'd study, but it would be something no one else in the family has done." I was embarrassed at my lack of precise direction, but Rory didn't seem concerned with the particulars.

"So do it."

"But how? Auntie Faye is too strong for me. It was all I could do to break away from her for this one day. Besides, she's planned I would go to Whitworth's from the day my mother died and started this entire mess." I felt angrier with my mother than I had ever let myself admit. Why, *why* had she sent me here? A small part of me even felt sorry for Auntie Faye. My mother had always been the thorn in her side. I looked at the fountain again. "Sometimes I do feel Auntie Faye wants what's best for me. Going against her seems wrong somehow."

"Don't make excuses for her," Rory said. "All Auntie Faye wants is control. She lost it over Ravenna and now she's trying it out on you. The woman is power mad. Anyway, if you were to move in a week from today, would that give you enough time?"

"I'm—I'm not sure."

As if he hadn't heard me, Rory said, "Next Saturday would be best."

"Who's telling Auntie Faye?"

"You are. You need to learn to stand up for yourself."

Chills went down my back. "I can't," I faltered.

"You can." Unconcerned, Rory set out a makeshift design with gravel in the grass.

"What do I say?"

"Tell her you've changed your mind about secretarial college. You think it's a waste of time and not what you want to do and you've decided to live in the city while you finish secondary school."

"I'm afraid."

"How can you be afraid? Auntie Faye is a paper tiger. There is absolutely no way she can stop you from making your own decisions."

Whatever Rory thought of Auntie Faye, my fear stayed with me, spoiling the rest of the afternoon and hastening my departure for home. But as I walked alone up the driveway, the wind shaking the sun-dried petals from the hydrangeas, I felt my worries dissolve. It was Rory making this decision for me, I reasoned, and I was just as powerless in the face of his will as I had been in front of my mother, Lily Parker, or Auntie Faye. I had let every one of them take over, but this time it was different: I didn't resent the interference, I depended on it.

Auntie Faye was setting the table for three with her second-best bone china when I walked into the dining room. I hadn't the nerve to explain that I wasn't hungry, making me wonder all over again how I would ever find the courage to break the news that I wanted to leave.

"Your uncle will be home in five minutes," she said. "It will be a pleasure for us all to eat together for a change. Have a nice day? Good. Now, I don't want to interfere, but I do hope you don't intend to spend too much time with Rory, dear. He isn't a suitable companion for you and the real danger as your uncle and I see it is that you might begin to think of him as more than a cousin. You know what I mean. Now go wash up for dinner."

"But I don't know what you mean."

Auntie Faye's forehead creased, but she continued laying out the silver. "You're not going to be obstinate about this, are you, Elizabeth? I'd have thought a Whitworth's girl would have more sense, more pride and ambition in life than wanting to hang around with a group of lazy students."

"Rory isn't lazy," I said, keeping my voice even. "He works very hard. In fact, Rory and I had a good talk today and I think it's time I started my own life and went to live with those 'lazy' students."

Auntie Faye put a spoon beside a gold-rimmed gravy boat. She turned to me, not a hair out of place. "Your uncle will be home any minute," she repeated calmly. "Let's not have him see us quarreling." She turned back to the table with an infuriating air of finality.

Steadying my voice, I said, "I can't forget about it because my mind is made up. I'm going next week."

"Elizabeth," Auntie Faye said, supremely patient. "I understand how necessary it is for you to exercise a bit of rebellion on occasion, but your timing is quite, quite wrong. I didn't want you to spend the day with Rory and this is why.

"Now will you please go get ready for dinner and give the potatoes a look on your way out. Here's your uncle at last." She arranged her features to match her table setting and held out her hands to Uncle Niall.

Uncle Niall walked into the room, his eyes flickering the briefest curiosity as I stormed past without any intent to check on the potatoes.

I closed my bedroom door behind me and leaned against the jamb, my thoughts chasing after me. I had done it. I had made the first move to cut through the restrictive bridle encircling my life and I was still alive. Amazing.

"Elizabeth, do hurry up," Auntie Faye called from the other end of the house.

I took a deep breath and returned to the dining room where she was in the middle of serving Uncle Niall. "The potatoes were nearly burning," she scolded as I took my place.

Uncle Niall gave us a perplexed look. "Have you had an enjoyable day?" he asked me.

"Yes, thanks. I went to an art gallery with Rory."

"So the boy is still determined to make his way with art?"

"He's having his own exhibition soon."

Uncle Niall buttered a piece of bread. "Is that right?"

Auntie Faye spooned peas onto my plate. "I'm sure there are more compelling topics to discuss than Rory."

"Of course there are," I replied, "if you let me get a word in edgewise."

"What's this?" Uncle Niall set down his bread and glanced around the table, ready to cauterize the first signs of infectious discord.

"I could throttle my brother," Auntie Faye said, showing her real anger at last. "I knew this would happen when I let Elizabeth traipse after Rory. He's trouble. Filling her head with absurd ideas. She hasn't told you all of it, either. Rory Haddon suggested she move in with him!"

"You make it sound terrible," I said. "I would simply be one of his flatmates. He's got scores of them."

"Don't exaggerate," Auntie Faye cut in.

Uncle Niall took a bite of veal cutlet. "What about Whitworth's?"

"I suppose she wants to quit."

"Quit?"

"I hate Whitworth's," I said. "I don't fit in and I never

wanted to go there, but everybody just assumed it would be the best thing for me. Well, it's not. I'd rather die."

"Really," said Auntie Faye. "You sound more and more like your mother every day." The insult stung.

"This is very unexpected," Uncle Niall said. "I never knew you were so unhappy at Whitworth's, or here, for that matter."

"Don't give in to her whims," Auntie Faye replied for me. "Your food is getting cold and I wanted you to have one peaceful meal this week." She turned to me.

"I don't know what to make of you lately," she said. "Always thinking of yourself and what you want. You've become impossibly selfish. You never go to see Clare—"

"Neither do you."

Peevishly, Auntie Faye fidgeted with her dessert spoon, and then pushed it away, disgusted. "You're not being fair," she said. "I am extremely busy running a household. Looking after you is just one more care at a time in life when your uncle and I should be relaxing. But instead we work very hard to keep you in Whitworth's. Once you've finished your studies you'll be grateful for the sacrifice we made."

"But I don't want to finish! Aren't you listening? Nobody's being fair to me. You let Ravenna have everything she wanted, so why can't I ask for this one little thing?"

"You're not Ravenna," Auntie Faye said as she did so often, only this time it was a mistake.

"Well, I'm sorry!" I shouted. "And whether you like it or not, I'm leaving. Tonight. Next week is too far away."

Frosty silence landed on the table with a thud, splashing the gravy and congealing the meat and potatoes into one icy, unappetizing lump. Raging against fate, I spun away from the table to the telephone in the hallway where I nervously dialed the number Rory had given me that afternoon.

Tania answered, making me feel small and ridiculous, but I had gone too far to turn back. "Is Rory there?" I heard her call his name.

"Hello?" He sounded tired.

"I'm sorry to bother you," I said quickly before I lost my nerve. "But I've had a monstrous row with Auntie Faye and I want to leave tonight. That is, if your offer is still open. I know it's sooner than you said." I felt a fool and the phone slipped in my damp hands.

A brief pause hung heavy on the line until Rory said, "Yeah, that'll be okay. There's just one problem. Can you get a bus?"

Relief made my legs buckle. He hadn't minded. "Of course," I said.

"Good. See you later, then."

I hung up the phone and rushed to my room where I made a mental list of what to take with me. There was very little I wanted. I put my books from Whitworth's in a pile on the dresser, counted out enough cash from my purse for the bus, and then packed the least offensive of my clothes, including the silk blouse Ravenna had given me before her wedding. The rest I left. I wavered over the silver heart in its pink box, but in the end I left that, too. I didn't want to be accused of stealing.

I came out of my room carrying my meager belongings in two plastic shopping bags just as Uncle Niall appeared from the dining room closely followed by Auntie Faye. "What's going on?" he asked.

"I should think it's obvious. I'm leaving."

Auntie Faye looked ready to explode. "Put those things down and we'll forget this ever happened."

"It won't make any difference."

Cold and mocking, Auntie Faye's eyes challenged me. "Do you seriously think you can support yourself living at Rory's?"

"He said he would help."

"Ah. He will help." She rocked back on her heels. "We'll see how long that lasts. In the meantime, you're being rash and impulsive and you will reproach yourself for this moment the rest of your life."

Uncle Niall quietly interrupted the steady stream of bile. He held out his hand. "Come and finish your dinner."

"Oh, don't try and stop her," Auntie Faye said. "She thinks she knows best. So be it. Wait until she finds out what life is like without the kindness of a family to fall back upon."

"Rory *is* family."

I focused on a spot somewhere between Uncle Niall and Auntie Faye where I couldn't see their faces, one ashamed and the other furious, and when nobody spoke, I went to the front door and walked out. It was over and I could barely contain the rush of deliverance I felt to finally head for the bus and the other side of kindness.

Rory and Tania were arguing in the kitchen when I arrived back at the flat. "She can't stay here," Tania was saying, an edge to her voice.

"She's got nowhere else to go."

I entered the room and no one tried to cover up the disagreement.

"Oh, great," Tania said when she saw me. "We'll probably be arrested for child abuse."

Rory glanced at my shopping bags. "Does Auntie Faye know you're here?"

I nodded. "I think she was actually glad to be rid of me."

Tania looked as though she sided with Auntie Faye. "Where are you putting her?" she asked Rory.

"I haven't worked it out yet." He turned to me. "Where would you like to be?"

"Anywhere. It doesn't have to be very big."

"Hmm. What about the sun porch?" Rory asked Tania. "There's an extra bed and mattress out back nobody's using, and I think there's a small table in the garage. A chair, too."

"It sounds fine," I said before Tania could say I was causing more sleepless nights than I was worth.

"Good. You can come and help me carry them in."

Rory and I dragged the bed and mattress he had spoken of into a tiny room tacked onto the side of the lounge. Tania brought an armful of mended sheets and blankets, and then pulled the faded curtains across three walls of glass.

"How do you like it?" Rory asked when we were finished.

"It's great."

"The bathroom's down the hall and turn right."

I tested the chair. "Thanks for letting me stay."

Rory smiled. "I have my reasons. Good night." He left with Tania and I was alone with what Ravenna had once called freedom. The sensation made me strangely light-headed and almost unwell.

The next few days I spent like an invalid. Without Whitworth's to attend, I slowly expanded into the routines of the household: sleeping late, reading in the bath, answering to no one but Rory. I sat for him most afternoons for which he paid me a small allowance that covered my expenses beyond room and board. I knew that at some stage I would have to pull my life together and figure out how to go back to school, but for now I felt as if I were recovering from a long illness.

Auntie Faye never called and I spent the better part of the day by myself, rarely encountering anyone other than Rory and Tania. I was aware of other people living in the house, their numbers varying by the week, but they were unimportant, shadowy figures usually at lectures or three-day tramping parties through the Waitakeres.

Rory had told me to use his studio any time I wanted, and I found myself gravitating toward the place when I had nowhere else to go. There I would try to understand the obscure canvases he had worked on the previous night, now spread around the room to dry. Unlike the conventional portraits he drew of me, these were strange, unpalatable things full of nightmare and tension, and like the vines growing through the windows, they began to creep into my dreams and being.

"The taniwha," Rory said when I asked. He held up a study in green and pointed to the semi-human, reptilian figure twined across the stretched fabric. "Are you telling me you've lived in this country for how long—nearly two years?—and you've never seen one?"

"I've heard about them," I said, remembering how frightened the stories had made Clare that long ago day on the beach. I looked more closely at the picture. "Why do you paint them?"

"I don't know. They intrigue me. Let's just say there's an element about them that appeals to my convoluted sense of relationships. Perhaps it's the way they just go after the female in question and steal her."

He handed me the picture, but I somehow missed the transfer and it slid between us. "Ravenna said something like that," I said, watching as he easily retrieved the painting and propped it against the wall.

"Ravenna? What would Ravenna know about the tani- wha? The taniwha is strong, a Maori symbol of strength and stealth, always hiding in the background, ready for ambush."

My eyes followed his and I noticed he had drawn the beast trapped and struggling in the depths of an ancient rain forest. The long neck twisted and raged while a heart of greenstone pounded through its entire body, refusing to surrender an inch of its life. It would be a matter of minutes before the taniwha thrashed free and trampled its unwary captors.

"Ravenna probably knows more about the taniwha than anybody," I finally said.

"Hey, when's the last time you were at Ravenna's, anyway?"

"Not since she got back from her honeymoon, months ago. She's in a world beyond me and Auntie Faye now."

Rory moved the taniwha to another wall. "You should go see her. Auntie Faye can't stop you, and besides, you don't get out of the house enough."

"Ravenna doesn't want to see me."

"You can't be so sure." Rory picked up a rag and began to scrub out a corner of the painting before he changed his mind and filled the area in again.

"What good would it do?" I asked. "Auntie Faye's probably turned her against me for good."

"Visiting Ravenna could do good for me and my exhibition. She'll think it's exciting, slumming with a pack of artists. Make her want to be part of things, make her bring her checkbook!"

I laughed. "Not Ravenna. She'll think the idea is either beneath her or completely mad. Or maybe Tania should ask. She spends all her spare time with Ravenna these days." I was surprised at the resentment I felt.

"Tania tried, and the truth is Ravenna flat out refused." Rory combed his fingers over his hair, leaving a smudge of green on his forehead. "Go on," he urged. "She'll listen to you. It would be unbelievably helpful if you could get her to bring her friends to my opening night."

"It sounds like you've got this all worked out. Maybe you should come with me."

Rory concentrated on his painting. "Ravenna and I are from two different worlds. I don't know her, not like you do." He gave the canvas one last appraisal and smiled. "Here," he said, giving it back to me. "It's yours."

I held it up to the window. The taniwha writhed across the moody terrain, and as much as it disturbed me, it had caught me and would not let me go.

Tania was raking leaves outside of Ravenna's house when I walked up the drive after an unhurried bus ride. In her jeans and a red polo-neck jersey, she was a much-needed sign of life on the bleak, bare-branched street. I waved to her with the rolled up sketch. I had decided to bring it at the last minute to show Ravenna an example of Rory's work, but Tania ignored me, making me more than a little self-conscious as I waited for the door to open. But when I at last heard high heels clicking along the marble tiles, I was again swept up into the glamour of Ravenna's presence and Tania seemed no more than the hired help.

"Elizabeth?" She opened the door a fraction wider. "What are you doing here? You should have phoned first. Mummy is having fits over you."

I looked at her black sateen trousers and the sleek new way she'd had her hair cut. "I'm sorry I didn't ring," I apologized, "but don't bring your mother into this. I had to get away from her. I had to!"

Ravenna held my shoulder and tried to hurry me into the house. "Come on," she said, her voice stern as she scanned the street. "Somebody might hear you."

"So what?"

"So everything. This isn't that kind of neighborhood." Without explaining what kind of neighborhood it was, she pulled me back to the room where she had served her mother and me coffee. A fire now blazed behind a brass screen and she motioned me toward a chair. "Get a hold of yourself," she said, "and ring Mummy. I know she'll forgive you and you can start over."

"I don't want to start over. I'm sick of trying to make her happy."

Ravenna sat down across from me and said, "Mummy 's on pins and needles about you."

"I don't feel guilty."

"No one is asking you to. But you should go home. This game has gone on long enough. Daddy talked to Whitworth's and they're being terribly understanding. They're keeping a place open for you."

"I'm not going back."

"You have to. You can't stay at Rory's forever."

"Why not? I like it there."

"You can't because you're sixteen years old and he's insane. It was absolutely wicked of him to let you stay in the first place. You're both lucky Mummy didn't get the police; it was all Alan could do to persuade her to leave you alone to cool off. And you have no idea how overworked he is." She passed me a box of tissues. "Here. Blow your nose."

I took the tissues. "Rory isn't insane," I said. "What have you all got against him?"

"It's nothing personal. It's his ideas we find so troubling. Look what he's done to you."

I couldn't stop my tears. "He hasn't done anything."

"Whatever, you can't stay with him. The whole mess is going to turn into a scandal any day now. Think of how this will affect Daddy, not to mention me and Alan!"

"It wouldn't be a scandal if I came here to stay with you."

Ravenna's poise faltered, and I quickly added, "I'd even go back to Whitworth's. You'd never have to see me."

Choosing her words carefully, Ravenna replied, "Of course it would be nice having you here, but I can't see where we'd put you."

"You have acres of rooms! Three stories worth."

Ravenna stood and leaned against the fireplace. "It's not the room."

I started shredding the tissues, dropping little pieces of fluff onto my lap. I didn't know why I had expected her to help me. "It's Alan, isn't it?"

"Partly." Ravenna frowned at the mess I was making. "Alan likes his privacy, and we're both so busy. Our lives are planned around set routines that can't be changed that easily. It's not that I don't want you; it's that Alan likes his life the way it is. Besides, it would look peculiar. People would still talk."

"Let them," I argued. "It might be good for them to look the taniwha in the face."

Ravenna turned and stared, hard. "The what?"

"Rory draws them." When Ravenna didn't answer I said, "He's got his own exhibition in a few weeks."

"I know. Tania mentioned it." She sighed. "She wanted money for it."

"He's a good artist. You might even find his work interesting if you gave it a chance. Look. I brought a drawing with me."

Ravenna waited as I knelt before the glass coffee table and unrolled the sketch. The taniwha almost leaped from the paper. She was about to comment when Tania entered the room, her red jersey and long, dark hair crackling with electricity when she saw me with the sketch. "Telephone," she announced, although I hadn't heard it ringing.

"Thank you." Ravenna left the room and I was alone with Tania.

She pointed to the drawing. "Where did you get that?"

"I took it from Rory's studio."

"Don't lose it." She looked like she wanted to say more, but she abruptly turned on her heel when Ravenna came back and sat down with another sigh.

"That," she said, reading a small piece of paper in her

hand, "was Wendy." She folded the note and tucked it behind a porcelain shepherdess.

"Wendy calls you?"

"Constantly. It's that precious job of hers. Always asking if Alan is here by any chance, as if he'd be home this time of day. Personally, I think she's checking up on me. I've tried to tell Alan, but he's always.... Oh, never mind. What were you saying about this exhibition?"

A clock chimed, loudly, stopping me from replying until it was finished. "I think Rory wants you at his opening night."

"Whatever for?"

"He thinks you and your friends might like to buy some of his work."

A little smile crossed her face before she rested her chin on her hand. "Why not?" she asked herself more than me. "I might even be able to bring the newspapers. Some friends, too."

"So you would go?"

She nodded, absorbed with the drawing she had minutes ago recoiled from. I couldn't wait to go back and tell Rory his plan had worked. I reached for the sketch, but Ravenna stopped me. "No, leave it here," she said.

I hesitated, remembering Tania's injunction. "So should I have Rory ring you with the details?" I asked.

"Fine. I'm not always home, but Tania can take a message."

I thought it ironic that Tania would take a message when

she could just as easily talk to Rory at the flat, but I said nothing as I pulled on my coat. Ravenna glanced up.

"We'll sort this thing out with Mummy," she said.

"It won't work."

"Yes, it will. Give me a few days to approach Alan. He'll know what to do." She returned to studying the drawing and I let myself out. Tania didn't seem to be around, a good thing when I didn't want her to see me leave empty-handed. I carried on by myself to the end of the street and then decided to walk the rest of the way home to save money.

I got back to the flat in time to catch Rory just as he was about to leave for a class. "Ravenna's going to do it!" I stepped back to watch his reaction.

"She's coming to my opening night?"

"With her friends and even the newspapers."

"Tania will be pleased." He glanced at his watch. "I'm in a hurry. See you later." He took off down the steps and passed by me, head down.

I watched him running away with my elation. I didn't know what I had expected from him: thanks, maybe praise, but his self-absorbed assurance unnerved me. I was swimming miles out of my depth, I thought. I didn't understand any of their motives, not of Rory or Ravenna or especially Tania. For an instant I felt the same as I had with Auntie Faye, like unnecessary, in-the-way clutter. And right now I suspected it was Tania who stood with the broom, ready to sweep me away if I made one more wrong move.

Chapter Twelve

While Rory's proposed exhibition took on paramount importance, Tania did her utmost to prevent my involvement in the affair. I had been the required bridge between Rory and Ravenna, and now my role was over. Now it was Tania who organized the twenty-five paintings in acrylic and oil for shipment; Tania who cleaned and readied the three collages; Tania who chose which of the five bronzes would be featured on the cover of the catalog. Like some high priestess of an exclusive, art-worshiping cult, Tania jealously guarded the flame of Rory's talent with a single warning: keep away.

"I know she's a Tartar," Rory said when I sounded him out on the subject, "but it's best to leave things to her and Ravenna. You can help out afterwards."

I watched him stretch and nail canvas over a frame for a new painting. "It's just that I feel I could do more than stay at home and wash the dishes," I said. "Maybe I should get a job."

Rory put his hammer down. "Wait a bit. After the exhibition you'll be so busy sitting for me you won't have time for a job. Things will be changing." He resumed his nailing and I knew if he said wait, I would wait.

But when Tania moved into the studio the day before the exhibition, I felt I had waited too long. Stuck in my sparsely furnished "sun room" listening to easels and cases being moved and rearranged to make room for Tania's belongings, each scrape along the floor tore at me. Life was going forward, and I felt left behind.

I watched the rain stream down the wide windows, rippling and distorting my emotions until I thought I would go mad. *Islands*, I thought, the rain beating in my ears like a grim pulse. Islands, tears, and the never-ending rain. I was ready to swim away if that was the only exit off this volcanic lump of jagged rock.

I remembered that the newspaper was delivered to the house every morning although no one had paid the bill for weeks or had the time to read it. I ran outside and found the latest edition lying with the other past issues rolled under the hedge where the delivery boy had thrown them. Keeping my coat over my head, I pulled the paper free, shook off the rain and mud as best I could from its plastic sleeve, and carried it dripping back to my room. There I peeled the sections apart until I came to "Situations Vacant."

I bit my thumbnail and skipped the appeals for secretaries and typists. The wet newsprint felt cold and pulpy in my hands and I knew I wasn't suited to nurse aiding. Not having a driver's license disqualified me from being a Girl Friday. Shop assistant would do. Anything would do. I scanned the columns asking for girls to train or work part-time in the waterfront tourist shops. Then I saw the ad for two junior assistants to work at Tyler's, a large bookstore in one of the newer arcades. The ad said you had to work a late night every week, but I figured that meant extra money. I began to want that extra money with the first real enthusiasm I had known for weeks.

I was at the store before ten-thirty. Fluorescent bulbs hummed noisily as the morning's customers queued up to buy magazines and business stationery. I approached a girl wearing one of the store's synthetic gray uniform smocks and asked if the job was still open.

"It could be," she said. With a book she summoned the manager to come over.

A woman similar to Auntie Faye, dressed in a sensible oatmeal twin-set and wearing the *de rigueur* pearls, hurried toward us. She stared at me for a second or two before asking, "What kind of work experience have you got? Ever work in a shop before?" She sounded like Auntie Faye, too.

"I was studying at Whitworth's," I said, "but I'd like a job where I could be out with people all day. The newspaper ad did say that the job was for a junior to be trained. And I love to read," I added. I thought my voice sounded shaky and unsure of itself.

The manager removed her glasses. "Whitworth's does produce good trainees," she said thoughtfully. "What's the capital of France?"

I wanted to ask what on earth that had to do with being

a junior assistant, but I dutifully replied, "Paris."

"America?"

"Washington, D.C."

We went on like this through a few more countries before she asked, "When can you start?"

"Today?"

She crossed her arms over her ample chest, deliberating. "Next Friday would be better." She then handed me an application form and asked what size of smock she should order.

After promising to be at the store at nine sharp next Friday morning, I thanked her and started the long walk home. I couldn't believe my luck. A bookstore was ideal. I had told the truth when I said I loved to read. Maybe I would just map out my own education through reading alone and forget about school. Apparently, I knew all that was required about geography. Holding my umbrella close, I was reminded of shipwreck survivors who started their journey back to civilization with the construction of a raft. This job would be my raft.

When I reached the gate to Rory's flat, I stood outside for a minute, letting water pour over my shoes. I could go back to England, I thought, if I earned and saved enough money. I tried not to worry about high airfares or that junior sales assistants earned next to nothing for their efforts.

"Don't stand out there—you'll catch your death!" Rory leaned out from the verandah, waving a paintbrush to attract my attention.

Reluctantly, I came back to reality and splashed my way up to where he stood beneath the eaves.

"Where have you been?" he asked, setting cleaned brushes along the wet railing. "I need you at the gallery this afternoon."

"Can't Tania help you?"

"Sure, but I need you, too. What are you doing wandering around in the rain?"

"Getting a job."

Rory rinsed a brush in a stream of rainwater rushing off the roof.

"I want to take care of myself," I said when I thought he wasn't listening to me. "I can do that now. Or I can after next Friday." I turned to head for my room. Uninvited, Rory tagged along behind me.

"I know I've made an absolute mess of things," he said easily.

"Why blame yourself?" I hung my coat on a hook as Rory sat on my bed, pulling his knees under his chin. "I'm glad to be here, away from Auntie Faye, and I'm glad to get a job. Everything's fine."

"It's Tania, isn't it?"

"What's my getting a job have to do with Tania?" I asked, mortified at his perception.

Rory leapt to his feet and began pacing the room, taking long, impatient strides cut off too quickly by the room's small dimensions. "Tania just sort of happened to me," he said. "We met in an art history class and, uh, she's very aggressive. Sometimes I don't even like her very much, but she's been incredibly supportive, and now she's acting as a gateway to Ravenna. Which is ridiculous when you stop to think Ravenna is my cousin, for God's sake. You'd think we could just talk without a go-between.

"By the way, do you know how much Ravenna has spent on food and drinks for tomorrow night?"

"No. No one tells me anything."

Rory shrugged. "It's a lot." He held in his breath for a moment, and then said, "I want to be a working artist, Elizabeth. I want to make a living from art, not teaching in some scummy second-rate school. I need a good first exhibition to get me started. One that's better than the usual student thing, one that will generate excitement. Ravenna's money can help me do that. I guess Tania felt entitled to some kind of commission."

He took in another breath and let it out again. "Where's this job?"

"Tyler's. The bookstore."

"Sounds terrible."

"I think it's great. I'll pay my share of the rent until I find somewhere else to live."

"You're not moving—"

"You're as bad as Auntie Faye. All you Haddons want control. No wonder my mother ran away."

"So you're keeping up family tradition?"

"No! Look, don't you have to be at the gallery?"

"I was waiting for you."

I looked around the small room. My bed was unmade and newspaper was strewn everywhere. In my haste to get to the store I hadn't eaten breakfast. Still, this was my first chance in a long time to be included with Rory's plans. "I need a few minutes to clean up and eat."

"Eat fast."

Rory left and I flattened the newspaper, glancing as I did so through the individual sections which seemed quite dry by now, until I came to the bottom of the fourth page: SUPERMARKET HEIR AND MAGNATE DEPARTS ON YEAR LONG SABBATICAL.

I skimmed the article, unable to comprehend what I was reading: Alan Trask, with what the writer considered good reason, was leaving New Zealand in pursuit of a year abroad traversing international golf courses. There was no mention of him taking his wife, in fact every indication pointed to the contrary.

A slow heat spread from my face to my fingertips, slightly moistening and disintegrating the edge of the paper as I read and re-read the clever mix of satire and factual, newsy reporting. It was all in there: Auntie Faye's plotting and scheming to catch her man; rumors of Ravenna's suspected and lost pregnancy; Alan Trask finally waking up to the millstone he carried in the form of our family and his screaming need to break free of us all by going abroad.

Like rows of barbed wire, the words twisted and scratched through our past, betraying truths we had each been determined, for private, separate reasons, to keep unexplored.

I found Rory in the kitchen with Tania. I poked the paper under his nose. "Read this." For once I didn't care what Tania thought of me. This didn't include her. She wasn't a Haddon.

Rory started to read the wrong headline about Pacific Rim currency fluctuations, but when I frantically pointed him to the right one, he tore the page away and sat on the table with enough force to almost knock it over. "How could he do this to me?" he groaned.

"Do what?" Tania peered over his head and tried to see what he was talking about.

"This!" Rory slapped the paper with the back of his hand.

She still couldn't find the story. "What's it say?"

"Oh, read it yourself." Rory slung the paper across the table and rubbed his eyes. "My show is going to be totally ruined," he mumbled. "This is the worst day of my life."

Tania found the article and she studied it from where it lay on the table. She let out a snort of frustration. "I knew Ravenna would blow it."

"Ravenna?" I said. "She didn't ask for this."

"Who asked you?"

"Lay off, Tania," Rory said. "It's over. The exhibition is finished."

Suddenly furious, Tania hit the table with her fists. "Okay, you want your exhibition over? Right. Then it's over between us, too." She glared at me and then back to Rory. "You can just go ahead and wallow with the rest of your greedy family."

Rory started to speak, changed his mind, and lurched from the kitchen. I could hear him as he pounded his way out into the rain.

Quivering with anger, Tania picked up the newspaper. "You brought this on," she said, her dislike of me underscoring the claim. "He never once mentioned any of you until you had the bright idea to move in. So you can move right out. You're too young to live here. You don't belong and the sooner you're gone the better."

Her words pierced me because I believed them, and reeling past her, I ran into the rain after Rory.

He sat beside an old Triumph motorcycle set on blocks in the unlit garage, a grease-covered chamois in his hands.

"I've got to talk to you," I said.

Tossing back his damp hair with a forced insouciance, he kept his gaze on the dirt. "We can talk."

"I wanted to say I was sorry."

"It's not your fault."

Rain sent a shower of rust from the corrugated iron roof down the windows. "I'm worried about Ravenna," I said at last. "What will happen to her? She'll never survive an attack like that, not alone for a whole year. Who knows if Alan's planning to ever come back?"

"You're asking what will happen to *Ravenna?*" He toyed with a spanner; the tight smile on his lips belied his show of indifference. "Ravenna has money. Money will pull her through anything." He looked out the window and added, "I know you think I'm using her. Perhaps I am. But she and everyone else in her crowd have made a lifestyle out of using people. I was simply cashing in."

"That makes it better?"

"It makes it realistic. Anyway, I probably don't have any chips left."

"With Alan gone, you can't be so sure Ravenna does either. I want to go to her."

Rory laughed in my face. "Very noble of you, but I don't think Mrs. Trask is seeing visitors today."

"She'll see me," I said, unwilling to share his cynicism. "I'll come to the gallery afterwards."

Rory threw the spanner into a toolbox where it fell with a dull clang. "Get in the van," he sighed.

A half hour later we pulled up outside Ravenna's house; the van glaringly out of place amongst the neighborhood Jaguars and BMWs. We ran up the steps, getting wet in the process. Rory rang the bell. Silence. "She's out," he said, looking past me out to the street.

"She's in there. Let's try around the back."

I took Rory to the back of the house, the wet flagstones glistening beneath our feet. A striped awning over the terrace had broken loose and the sound of it flapping in the wind sent a shiver through me. Ravenna had to be in. "Try the windows," I said.

Rory walked the length of the house, thumping at the

shutters with the flat of his hand and calling Ravenna's name until at last an upstairs light flashed on. We looked up to see Ravenna haloed against her bedroom window. When she saw us, she motioned for us to meet her at the kitchen door.

Once she was downstairs she silently opened the door as if we were beggars. Her greeting was no warmer than what we had left outside.

"Thanks," Rory said, dripping both rainwater and sarcasm before blowing on his hands.

A storm of emotions crossed Ravenna's face: fear, indecision, outright hostility.

"Don't be angry," I said when she didn't speak. "I want to help."

"With what?"

"We read the paper this morning."

Ravenna bolted the door and tested the handle. "Oh, about Alan, you mean? He's off to investigate golf courses. He's thinking of building a chain of resorts once he gets back. It's quite a brilliant decision...."

We stood on her intricate tiled floor shedding water until Ravenna said, "You shouldn't have bothered to come here."

Lightly, I reached for her arm and felt the fear beating inside her like a trapped bird. "It was my idea," I said. "I didn't think you'd want to be alone."

Dredging up a shadow of her past talents, Ravenna feigned a reasonable show of surprise. "I'm not in any danger!" She turned to Rory. "Why aren't you at your gallery hanging pictures? I spent a lot—way too much money on tomorrow night. It had better go well."

Rory gave her a wry grin. "There's really an opening night?"

"Of course there is. Don't be so silly." Ravenna took a towel from a hook and bent down to wipe up the rainwater just like her mother so often did. "Listen, it's very touching of you to want to 'rescue' me or whatever this is, but I'm fine. Absolutely fine." Just then the phone rang and her reaction reduced her brave words to dust.

The noise continued for twelve more rings while Ravenna stood stock-still. When the last ring died, she sank into a nearby chair. "They can't make me talk to her," she said, her voice quaking. "I won't talk to Wendy, not even if she calls me a hundred times a day."

It dawned on me that Wendy could very well have been the "inside source" the article had referred to so carefully.

"Do you want me to talk to her?"

"Go with Rory," Ravenna whispered. "I told you; I'm fine."

For an instant the anguish in her eyes was so apparent I wanted to fling my arms around her and demand she come away with me. We had both been pawns of Auntie Faye; the difference was I had been a piece from a mismatched set and thereby easy to lose. I put my hand on Rory's sleeve. "Wait for me in the van. I won't be long."

"Five minutes."

I waited for the door to close behind him and then said, "Just come back to Rory's flat with me for a little while. We can have lunch and you can forget Wendy and everyone else for a few hours."

"What do you mean, 'forget'?" she asked sharply. "Nobody's ever going to forget. All people want to do is remember. They make the rules and you have to follow them, and even that isn't good enough most of the time."

"Then why try to please them now?"

She didn't answer and I tried to understand what she might have been thinking. "Didn't Alan tell you he was going away?"

The question startled her. "How could he have? I was too busy learning my lines. There wasn't any time to know what he was doing. But that didn't matter to anyone else, did it? No, it was sit back and watch Ravenna bring on the show. Now the show's over. Time for Ravenna to go back in her box."

"How can you talk about yourself that way? There was never any show, never any box, at least not as far as I was concerned." I searched her face for some sign from the past I could recognize. "There was just you being perfect and us wanting to be like you." My throat caught for an instant. "I still do."

Ravenna pushed my words away. "You won't. Not after this."

Her acceptance of the situation infuriated me. "Why make an absurd newspaper article full of lies sound so important?" I shouted, wheezing as I thought I could somehow clobber her into reason. "Who's going to believe it, anyway? And what does it matter if they do?"

"It matters."

"No, it doesn't. It can't." Again I wanted to go to her, but as though sensing my approach, she lowered her head and blocked me out completely. The moment was lost. I didn't wait to say good-bye.

Chapter Thirteen

Back in the van on the way to the gallery, I tried to tell Rory what Ravenna had said and what I felt. "It's so weird. Where was everyone? The street was *empty*. I would have thought Auntie Faye would be there making tea or fending off reporters."

"Maybe that was her trying to reach Ravenna." Rory looked away from the traffic for a second. "If you ask me, no one was there because it's a load of rubbish. Either that or no one can afford the taint of being part of the 'out' crowd. Including Auntie Faye. In her eyes, if Alan leaves Ravenna, then both Auntie Faye and Ravenna have failed.

"Anyway," he said, "Frank's going to have a seizure if Ravenna keeps up this seclusion act."

Frank was the owner of the gallery. A balding, soft-spoken man in his early forties, he had been introduced to me as "the guy who knows everything." I thought he'd been calm enough with the moniker, but when Rory and I now entered the gallery through the delivery doors he was every bit as agitated as Rory said he would be.

"Get a grip," Rory told him as soon as we were pacing

down a length of newly laid parquet flooring. Our heels echoed off the shiny, unscarred surface; the sound of possible scuff marks seemed to increase Frank's worry load.

"Rory," he said, "most of the pictures haven't been unwrapped and no one has told me what they want done with the bronzes." Frank looked at me without recognition. "Where's Tania?"

Rory shrugged—a quick, dismissive gesture—and ran his hands over the bleached hessian on the walls. He flicked imagined dust from the fibers. "She's at home. What happened to those instructions she typed up for you?"

Frank's features slid deeper into depression. "Lost. Can't find them anywhere." Lowering his voice, he added, "And if the papers are correct, we've lost the lovely Mrs. Trask and friends. What a catastrophe."

"Pure speculation," Rory replied, adjusting the angle of a lamp. As he spoke, Frank's receptionist leaned out of his office, holding a telephone receiver. "Frank—it's for you," she said.

Frank went to his office to take the call, and I looked around the faddish, sterile gallery. It was the right setting for an exhibition that now seemed as stunted and thwarted in time as the bonsai trees grouped on every available surface. "You don't need those instructions," I said.

Rory brushed more dust from the hessian. "You're right. I've been designing the lay-out in my sleep." He started to take some hand measurements of the walls. "Okay," he said, "since it's just you and me, be a good girl and do as I tell you."

I set my apprehensions about Ravenna on hold and did as Rory asked: carrying, hanging, and re-hanging the thirty-three pieces that made up the collection of his best work. When we were finished, Frank stepped back out to share in our sense of achievement.

"It's sheer genius," he said, his mood much improved. "This mass portrayal of—what can I say? The power of despair. It's flawless. Absolutely flawless."

Rory straightened a scene of the taniwha leering from behind a house on fire. "Let's just hope it sells."

Frank winked in my direction. "Artists," he groaned.

The next morning and the first day of the exhibition arrived with a cold mist and another newspaper. Search as I might, I couldn't find a single follow-up mention of Alan Trask or his proposed leave of absence. Neither could Rory when I gave him the paper, interrupting his breakfast of cold toast and tea.

From the other side of the kitchen, Tania offered her own explanation for the oversight. "He's old news," she said, slapping bread into the toaster.

Rory tipped the remains of his tea out the window and gave Tania an angry, perplexed glare. "Where were you yesterday?" he asked her.

"I do have classes to attend every now and then."

"So do I, but I thought we'd agreed to meet at the gallery."

"You could have fooled me."

Not wanting to be part of this latest disagreement, I left them arguing and shut myself away with a book. For the next forty minutes I could hear doors banging and people leaving the house for lectures. Finally silence reigned, and I ventured out of my room to examine the wreckage. The house was the same as most days: unwrapped bread left to dry out on the kitchen table, laundry thrown in piles around the lounge, a stereo amplifier hissing with nothing set up to play, its beady red eyes angrily demanding the thing be turned off. I pulled the plug, made myself some toast, and went back to my book.

By the time six o'clock rolled around, Rory finally came home. "I'm just back to take a shower," he announced. "I'll be leaving after that if you want a lift." He picked up my book. "Since when did you start reading Camus?"

I ignored the question. "What about Tania?"

"Your guess is as good as mine. If she doesn't show up soon we'll have to go without her."

"We could wait."

"No. If she wants to sulk, that's her choice." He turned toward the bathroom.

I had decided days ago what to wear: new jeans I'd bought from the money Rory paid me and the silk blouse Ravenna had given me before her wedding. I hardly ever had a reason to wear it, and until yesterday, tonight was intended to be a major celebration. The feel of the fabric was luxurious against my skin and created a comfortable barrier between me and what I envisioned could now be a potentially embarrassing evening. Especially when I felt I had no real right to be there.

Lights and music streamed from the gallery windows as we approached the side street entrance. Frank lounged in the doorway, a drink in one hand, an exhibition catalog in the other. He raised his glass in greeting. "The caterers were on time, thank God. Pity Mrs. Trask won't be."

Glancing over Frank's head to the throng inside, Rory took a sip from Frank's drink. "Great. No Tania and no Ravenna. Their loyalty astounds me."

Frank ushered us inside and the rest of Rory's complaints were drowned by the enveloping surge of his art school friends.

"Rory!" A dozen girls elbowed their way past the elegantly clad guests on what appeared to be the "Ravenna side" of the room. Throwing themselves into Rory's arms, they screamed, "It's fantastic! We knew you could do it!"

Rory beamed them a mechanical smile and headed straight for the bar. Trailing in his wake, I couldn't help hearing the snippets of snide conversation bouncing from wall to wall: "They say Trask has gone for good. Yeah, he's left his wife. No, she won't be coming tonight. How could she?"

My hand shook as I reached for a bottle of mineral water. I tried to pour a small amount into a silly plastic goblet without splashing the woman next to me. Her voice, an irritating, high-polished whine, rose out of her low-cut evening gown and circled endlessly around a single theme.

"I never did know what to make of Ravenna Trask," she said to a woman on her other side. "She has no real breeding to speak of. They say Alan found her decorative."

I couldn't listen any more. Dizzily, I made my way to the door in a futile quest for fresh air, but more and more people were arriving, shouting Rory's name in greeting and then getting into the thick of things to admire the paintings while tearing Ravenna apart at the same time. The two names blended into a rumbling roar: *Ravenna, Rory; Rory, Ravenna....*

My eyes stung from tears, cigarette smoke, and the flashy strobe lighting against the back wall. I turned around in time to see Rory pull his shirt over his head and toss it into a corner. Frank stooped to pick it up, his smile straining at the creases. Someone spilled a bottle of wine as another crowd popped in, shouting that they were from the university's engineering department and didn't give a hoot for fine art but they heard there were free drinks going. Frank began to put red "sold" stickers beside a number of paintings. The evening, I surmised, was going well.

Sometime around midnight the party came to an abrupt halt when Frank turned off the overhead lights and music, and announced the bar was closed; it was time to comply with the law and shut the gallery. To the sound of assorted moans of disgust, Frank chucked out the last art student who left laughing on the arm of a man dressed in a tuxedo. The doors closed after them and Rory slumped over a table, his hands to his eyes. "God, I feel bad," he mumbled.

Frank stood over him. "You need some sleep."

"Can I just crash on the floor somewhere?"

"The floor—the *new* floor—is covered in glass. I'll give you a lift. It's the least I can do for a not-so-struggling young artist. You can pick up your van tomorrow." Frank ducked into his office.

Rory started to button his shirt and getting it wrong, started all over again, then gave up and left it hanging open. "How many did we sell?" he shouted to Frank.

Frank came back with his jacket and keys. "Enough for your first night. I've also had a substantial offer for the bronzes." He looked at me as if he'd just noticed me for the first time. "Can I drop you off somewhere?"

Before I could speak, Rory said, "She's staying at the flat."

Frank nodded a little too knowingly for comfort, and we followed him out to the car. "Not a bad night, after all." He unlocked the passenger doors. "Ravenna Trask was still able to pull in the money."

"Thanks to her husband," Rory said sourly. He struggled over me into the front seat and I got out to make room for him. When he didn't budge I settled for the back.

Frank started the engine. "Think he's staying overseas?"

Whatever Rory said, I didn't hear, but it made Frank laugh. We drove without further conversation for another mile or so, when Rory put his hand firmly on the steering wheel at the next set of traffic lights. "You can drop us off here," he said. "We'll walk the rest of the way."

"If you're sure…."

"I am. Hey, I'll see you tomorrow when I get the van. We can talk about a deal for those sculptures."

Frank pulled up to the curb and this time Rory helped me out of the car. He saluted Frank before he drove away. I stretched my legs; my right foot had gone to sleep. "Why did you want to walk home?" I had no idea where we were and it was cold.

"I couldn't stand being cooped up in the car any longer. All night I've felt caged."

"I thought you were having a good time. And you did sell a lot of paintings." I shivered and wrapped my arms around my waist.

The cold meant nothing to Rory. "Trust me, people didn't buy for the sake of art," he said. "Every time I tried to talk about my work to someone other than my art school friends, you'd think I was discussing a blank wall for all the interest they showed.

"Can you believe what one woman said to me? 'Very ornamental. Very sweet.' Sweet? Pictures of earthquakes and forest fires? It took me a full fifteen minutes to realize she was referring to those bloody bonsai trees!"

I had to walk fast to keep up with Rory's outraged stride. "You're the one always saying you've got to sell," I reminded him. "What difference does it make why people buy the work?"

Rory slowed down so I could catch up to him. "There isn't a difference in the long run, I know, but, it's just—

just—" He searched for the words and gave up.

"Funny, wasn't it?" he asked instead. "How Ravenna was the center of attention and she wasn't even there?"

A wind blew past us, rustling the trees. "Ravenna was born to be the center of attention," I said.

"And we're just a couple of outcasts. Rebels in the Haddon clan. Maybe we'll be disowned."

"What for?"

"Thinking our own thoughts? Going our own way?"

"You, maybe," I told him. "So far I've just made everyone think I need to be committed to an institution." I looked up and down the unfamiliar street without recognizing any of it. "Where are we?"

"If you're upset about Tania," Rory said, passing over my question, "I'd disregard three quarters of everything she says. Letting her move into the studio was a supreme miscalculation on my part."

A few threads of moonlight sifted through a cloudbank and I knew where we were. "Don't you think it's a little late to go bother Ravenna?"

"I want to know how she and Tania spent their evening. It must have been one laugh after another."

I felt a chill in the air that spoke of more than a late fall night crawling into winter. It was the edge of an over-sharp blade, its oily sheen smelling of ice and lighter fluid, bringing on the first wave of nausea before unconsciousness; it was my mother as I thought of her laid out broken in the muddy snow.

I didn't want to know anything about Ravenna. My ribs constricted and my feet became clumsy and rigid. It was too soon; it was too late; it would wait until morning.

"I don't want to know," I whispered after him, but Rory was already running up the walkway to her house.

The door flew open under his knuckles and I backed away when Tania appeared on the threshold, her hair hanging loose and her face smeared and dirty.

Grabbing Rory with hands like claws, the words tumbled out of her: "Something's wrong with Ravenna—I don't know what to do—I don't know what I did!"

Chapter Fourteen

I t took Rory a minute to react, and then he only said, "Where is she?"

"Her bathroom. Hurry! I don't understand what's happened. We were talking and then she left to go upstairs and didn't come back." Tania tightened her grip, pulling Rory closer. "You have to help me."

Rory pushed her away and began hurling doors open. Nothing. Like a stage-set, the furniture waited for the visitors who would never come again. He started for the stairs in frustration. "Why haven't you rung anyone?"

"The phones aren't working. They're disconnected or turned off or something."

Clinging to the banisters, I followed Rory up the staircase, guided by Tania's incessant flow of guilty chatter.

"I came to work as usual. I always work Fridays," she panted. "And Ravenna didn't feel like going to the exhibition right away. She started to go through her clothes, pulling everything out of the closet, and then she got angry and brought out her wedding dress in a stupid plastic bag that said some rot about 'Marriage is Forever' and she started tearing strips of lace off it. I don't know why, maybe I was angry with Alan, too, he's such a creep, but I started helping her. We tore off the sleeves—"

The last door gave way to Rory's fury and there was no going back. Ravenna lay beside her marble bathtub, her eyes closed and her head pillowed on a filthy lace skirt. Next to her extended, mottled hand, was the damning newspaper article, neatly clipped and ready for Auntie Faye's scrapbook: *Supermarket Heir Departs*.

Water dripped from the gaping, senseless mouths of the gold dolphin taps, and I remembered Auntie Faye's reaction the first time she had seen them: "Never in my wildest dreams."

Instinctively, I bent over Ravenna to wake her, to force open her eyes and make her rise to a sitting position. "Ravenna?"

"Don't touch her."

My gaze shot up to meet Rory's eyes in a mirror. The reflected pain magnified itself through repetition until we both could stand no more and we looked to where Tania pounded on yet another set of mirrors, directing us to the message written in the middle in grape-red lipstick above our heads.

"I don't know why she wrote it. I didn't do anything except keep her company and pour out a couple of drinks. I didn't give her anything else. I don't know where she got the pills; her father's a doctor, isn't he? I didn't give them to her. So why should she want to write my name? Why would she blame me?"

"Stop it!" Rory hit her so hard against the wall she didn't have time to cry out before a little trickle of blood left her lips and she sank to the floor.

"I don't know why she wrote it."

Tani

Trembling, I read each letter separately, sounding out the possibilities until I knew for sure. My mouth was dry as I lifted the smashed lipstick from the floor and placed it gently upon a shelf next to the sink. "It doesn't say...it doesn't say what you think."

"I don't care what the hell it says," Rory spat at me. "Just get help. Go on! Get somebody—anyone—but get help."

My ears ringing, my feet numb, it finally sank in that Rory meant me and when he raised his hand as though to hit out again against this awful thing none of his violence could ever make right, I ran.

There was no time to think. I was running to the kauri staircase, which seemed to go down a long, long way, longer than I remembered, and I managed to open the front door, but then I stopped. My task overwhelmed me; I didn't know where to begin. Every door seemed locked, every curtain drawn, every back turned. The entire street was closed to me, as if to say, "You should never have come here in the first place. *You should never have come.*"

But I was here and I had to go on. I slid across the wet

grass to the house next door and yelled for admittance, longing for the smells and sounds of early morning normalcy. I wanted people in thick terry dressing gowns, with coffee percolators and boiled eggs, and most of all, I wanted pardon, for I blamed myself. I should never have left Ravenna alone.

A woman opened her door as far as the brass chain holding it back would allow. A noise rattled in my throat. "Ravenna," I whispered, motioning which house I had come from. "She's not breathing."

"And?"

"I need you to call an ambulance, the police, anyone. You've got to."

The woman took the chain off its hook, as though weighing the cost of her assistance. *You should never have come.*

"Go back to the house," she said. "I will ring the police." She closed the door and I heard the brass chain return to the hook. With nowhere else to go, I returned to Ravenna's front steps to wait for whatever assistance would be arriving.

I stayed outside, unable to enter the house alone. I couldn't bear to go back upstairs. The cold snaked its way around me as I went over all the "if-onlys" that might have prevented this nightmare. If only Ravenna had let me move in with her; if only she had never married Alan Trask; if only we had never been born.

A stream of sirens arrived one after the other, each competing for an attention no one on the street would lower their guard to acknowledge. A beacon light atop the ambulance pointed me out to the police and they followed me inside.

Rory and Tania were crouched on the bathroom floor when we entered. Slowly, Rory rose and handed the officer in charge the newspaper cutting. The man gave it a cursory glance and then stepped aside to let the ambulance team do their work; it was clear there was no need to rush.

The same officer who accepted the paper started to lightly finger the smudged lipstick on the mirror before realizing we were all three staring at him. He moved his finger to the side of the unfinished message and tapped the glass. "What is this?" he asked, looking as he spoke at Tania's bruised and bloodied mouth.

I felt I was taking part in a film; nothing was real. A blanket mysteriously appeared as if from the air and swathed itself across Ravenna's vacant face. Tania held a towel to her mouth and started to cry again while Rory's eyes bored holes into me, willing me not to say another word. But someone had to let the monster free.

"What is the—?" Again, the officer tapped the glass with his square fingernail.

"Taniwha," I said, disregarding Rory's frown. My lips and tongue swelled full of riverbanks and small black, scaleless fish. I needed to spit them out.

"Why? Some kind of code?"

A childhood scar I had never noticed over Rory's left eyebrow reddened suddenly, but he said nothing, and the officer shrugged when one of the ambulance crew passed him the empty prescription bottle. Absent-mindedly, he slipped it into his pocket and then waited for one of us to reply.

"It doesn't mean a thing," I said when no one else spoke. I could tell it was a most unsatisfactory answer.

The police station was quiet for an early Saturday morning. The arrests from the night before were asleep in their cells and the phones rang haphazardly without urgency. Suffocated by the chipped plaster horror of the place, I barely had the strength to wonder who had been the most frightened of the taniwha: Ravenna or Auntie Faye? Or me?

But it was time to give my statement. I think the police found me particularly disappointing. I would not explain the reason for Ravenna calling to the taniwha. I could not tell them the whereabouts of Alan Trask. No, I did not know where he went. No, Ravenna did not speak of him. No, twenty times no. I could not summon him up on demand. Alan Trask had become the ultimate negative. They would have to ask Ravenna's parents for information, I said. The police said they would like Rory and me to be there when they did, but Tania would be detained until further notice. There were more questions to ask her, more monsters to pull out of the dark.

I don't remember anything about the drive to Auntie Faye's except the sun was shining brilliantly. The police spoke low and opened doors for us, treating us with mild efficiency, politely ignoring Rory's wall of insolence in order to complete their official duties.

We stood in a group inside the doorway. While the police tunneled through Auntie Faye's incomprehension (*"There must be some mistake. I don't understand. She was so happy."*) I noticed how much larger the garden had become in one season. Everything was growing outward and away, tumbling down to the sea in a mass of green.

"My God, my God…." Auntie Faye's screams ripped the wintry air, bringing Uncle Niall, dressed for his Saturday golf game, to her side. He looked at the police, looked at us, and promptly became a professional, leading us away from the neighbors' hearing; calming, soothing, comforting on the strength of habit.

The police used words like "tragedy," "overdose," and "weak constitution," but I couldn't hear them properly. Not with Auntie Faye's dry heaves and Rory scowling like he hated every one of us.

"You have no idea where Alan Trask could be?"

Auntie Faye shoved her grief away with surprising rigor. "Alan Trask is of no concern to us," she said. "My daughter's death cancels out all obligations we might ever have held to the man." Looking directly into the face of law and order, she said, "Alan Trask killed my child."

The police did not argue, asking instead, "Is there anything further we can do for you?" They spoke quickly to save time; they had to get back to their clean world of reports and discernible facts.

"Thank you, no," said Uncle Niall. "I will notify the rest

of my wife's family. When will it be possible to see my daughter?" His voice came through perfectly controlled. Uncle Niall had dealt with death before.

An answer was given and the police left us free to throw the first of many stones. A current passed between Uncle Niall and Auntie Faye and shielding his eyes from the yellow glare of sunlight, Uncle Niall asked, his voice no longer so proficient, "You found her?"

I moved closer to Rory. "Yes."

Auntie Faye gripped the window ledge behind her. "Too late," she reminded me. "You were too late."

"I couldn't help it—she wanted to be alone—"

Rory broke in: "Stop apologizing. She doesn't deserve an explanation."

"But I want to tell her." The emotions I had kept bottled inside for the last seven hours were beginning to take shape: heart of greenstone; the shimmering curl of emerging fern; Ravenna dancing along the shore, promising me happiness. Would anyone ever understand?

Rory placed himself between Auntie Faye and me. "They don't want to hear," he said, and then added, "I'm going back. If you want to come with me it'll have to be now."

Appalled, Uncle Niall shook his head. "No, not yet. She won't say it, but your aunt needs you." Hesitantly, he approached her, but Auntie Faye declined his comfort and turned toward the window, her face as salt-tempered and eaten with despair as a battered figurehead.

Rory made his hands into fists which he stuffed into his jacket. "Let's go," he said.

No one tried to stop us.

It felt strange to be on the street again; strange to be amongst people starting a day Ravenna would never know. Rory looked at me from the corner of his eye as we headed for a bus.

"What were you thinking last night?" he asked.

I had thought of a hundred different things.

"You know, about the taniwha.'"

I kept my eyes focused on the road. "There's no great mystery to it."

"But you think it's my fault? Because of my drawings?"

"It's nothing to do with you. If anyone's at fault, it's Alan Trask. Or Auntie Faye. Or maybe it's our grandparents for dying young."

Rory was quiet for a few minutes before he looked back at me. "I'm not going to the flat," he said.

"Where, then?"

"The gallery. I want to tell Frank to stop the exhibition, to close it down. I feel like I never want to paint again."

I stopped walking, heedless of the passers-by on their way to work and the morning paper. "So you'd let the Haddons kill you, too," I said. "Wonderful. Perhaps we should all kill ourselves, the sooner the better. Obviously it would save a lot of time and effort if we got it over and done with—"

A woman pushing a pram missed me by inches.

"That's not the point!" Rory shouted. "I don't want to die. I want to live and I can't! Not like before. I feel used up, like there's nothing left of me. I feel tired and lonely and sick of everything, especially my work."

"How can you say that?" I asked, lowering my voice. "We're Haddons. We're meant to carry on."

"Haddons," Rory said, flagging down the bus. "What have we ever made worth keeping?"

I had no ready answer.

There were no invitations to Ravenna's funeral; just a phone call from Auntie Pat to tell me where to be, what to wear, and not to notice Auntie Faye's increasingly strange behavior.

"I never do," I told her, but Auntie Pat pretended not to hear, and she returned to appearances, stressing the importance of dressing to suit the occasion.

"Jet beads, black crape, that sort of thing?" I asked.

"Oh, Elizabeth," she sighed from her house turned hospital across the bay. "This is not a time to joke."

Neither, I said, was it a time for grief. At least not for me. Similar to when I heard the news of my mother's death, my emotions were something to put away for the future, like good clothes. There was no way I could fall into some shrieking, gaudy display when I was well-used to wearing death's stifling, scream-proof garment. But again, Auntie Pat pretended not to understand.

The days spent waiting for the funeral spilled out slowly. As the service was scheduled for the following Friday, I lost the job I was never able to start. Tania kept out of sight, and Rory kept to his word. He did not paint, but took to drawing in charcoal and a shade of violet crayon with some unpronounceable, unhappy name I cannot remember. Day and night merged into one for him as he leaned for hours over his drafting table, his long hair hiding his face and his left hand scuttling across the expensive paper he invariably destroyed. It was impossible to save those dreams he no longer shared with me. Once I stood in the doorway and watched until the tea I brought him grew cold and filmy in my hands. But it was no good; Rory did not turn around. He did not want anything that wasn't black, gritty, and morbid.

Auntie Pat drove into the city by herself to take us to the North Shore ceremony. Dressed in a frayed, outdated black wool suit that pinched under the arms, she bore the bulk of the family's guilt like a penitent. Guilt prevented her from speaking too loudly and guilt made her choose to humbly remain in the car while I was sent to fetch Rory.

I hadn't seen him all that morning, and the door to his studio was shut. I stood outside in the hall and heard the radio and the underlying sound of Rory and Tania talking.

"Rory? Tania?" I called. "We have to leave. Auntie Pat's waiting in the car."

After a moment or two, Tania, wrapped in a sheet, opened the door. "We're not going," she said.

I looked past her bare shoulder and saw Rory half-asleep, sprawled across his mattress, a cigarette between his lips.

"Auntie Pat's here," I told him from the hall, unwilling to cross into their mutual, disturbing territory. "You'll have to hurry."

Rory's voice was as cold as the chilly hallway. "I went to Ravenna's wedding," he said. He yawned and tapped ash into a stone bowl on the floor beside him. "My family debts are paid."

"This isn't for Ravenna. It's for me."

Rory lifted his head. "I'm sorry, but there's nothing left in me for you to want. Nothing." He held out his empty hand, spreading his fingers apart and letting all the warmth I needed fall through.

I hesitated, and Tania gave me a look of pity mixed with an unspoken, "You see?" that sent me back to the car and Auntie Pat without them.

"Where's Rory?" she asked. "And that girl. Tania, is it?"

I slid into the front seat beside her. "They're not coming," I said. I was glad she had stayed in the car. I didn't want to explain Tania's shoulders or the ragged sound of Rory's voice.

Auntie Pat didn't pester me with any further prying, but when she had turned off the bridge, she said, "It's too bad about Rory. Faye won't like having an empty place at the service. It's irksome enough Morgan and Sheena can't get off that blessed farm and as for Alan Trask…."

She stopped for a red light and passed me a toffee. "On the other hand, Faye will probably be relieved to have Rory gone. She can't bring herself to forgive him for finding

Ravenna like that."

"I was there, too." I bit down on butterscotch.

"Faye is angry with you for other reasons, though she wants you there all the same."

"You can't win with Auntie Faye."

"No," she agreed. "You can't."

We pulled into Auntie Faye's driveway and parked behind a line of three standard issue black funeral cars. Hired drivers stood by each vehicle. Their shiny suits, thinning hair, and widely spaced teeth set them apart, like a family of eerie triplets.

We were late, arriving just in time to see Uncle Niall guide a procession out of the house and toward the assembled cars. Dressed in tasteful cream and navy with gold nautical buttons, Auntie Faye walked beside him, her entire weight deposited on his arm, and he had some trouble keeping her upright while he assigned us to our drivers.

"Faye and I will ride in the first car," he instructed the clustered mourners when I heard the crunch of wheels on gravel behind me. I turned and saw Uncle Brian pushing Clare in a wheelchair.

"Next," Uncle Niall continued, "I thought Pat, Brian, and Clare could go in the second car, followed by Wendy, Elizabeth, and Rory in the third." Auntie Pat started to pantomime Rory's absence, and he stopped. "Rory isn't here? Oh. Well, then. It would be a great help if Wendy and Elizabeth could take Clare's chair with them."

As though walking through some deadly fog, we then

started for our designated places, the other less culpable guests providing their own transport. One of the triplets held a car door open for me and I climbed inside, Wendy right behind me, dragging Clare's collapsible wheelchair after her.

When the door closed with a soft swish of air, she said, "I didn't expect to see you here."

"I could say the same about you."

We didn't speak for a few minutes and Wendy finally asked, "Where's Rory?"

"Home."

"Is it true he's living with that girl? The one who—"

"She didn't do anything," I said, trying to be fair. I looked at Wendy more closely and found myself despising everything about her: her hair, the flowery perfume I could have sworn was Ravenna's favorite; even her prissily-manicured nails riled me. "It's none of your business why Rory and Tania aren't here, but they're not hypocrites. I don't recall you ever having any great love for Ravenna. Or has unemployment put you at a loose end and you had nothing better to do than come and sniff out some new stories for the papers?" I turned my head away as our car started to coast down the drive after the others, and Wendy grabbed the handles of the wheelchair when it started to slide onto our feet.

"What makes you think I'm out of work?" she asked, propping the chair against her bony knees. "Alan might be overseas, but the business hasn't closed down. Far from it.

Food sales have never been higher. And for the record, I had nothing to do with those stories. I'm here because Mum asked me to be."

I didn't believe her, but I was too tired to argue. After a minute, Wendy spoke up again. "They don't normally bury suicides in consecrated ground." It was too much.

"What would you have preferred?" She *was* wearing Ravenna's perfume. "Placing her at the crossroads with a stake through her heart?"

Wendy didn't answer, but instead kept her eyes and hands on the wheelchair, rubbing the handles to a greasy shine. I leaned my head back and as if it were my own life closing, the whole of the short time I had loved and admired Ravenna played through my mind, scene by abbreviated scene. I thought of her on her wedding day, balanced on a tightrope of decorum that never slackened. Yes, we were enthralled by her. Amused, fascinated, in competition with her. But had any of us ever known her?

The car slowed down and we drove through some land developer's idea of heavenly rest: iron gates, swaying cypresses, and a modern sculpture in the form of an abstract and oversized harp.

When the car stopped, I left Wendy to the chore of delivering the wheelchair to her parents, and taking my time, I walked to where the earth was cut open in a tidy plot, ready to receive Ravenna at her last social engagement.

I found a seat where I could think my own thoughts away from the censure of Auntie Faye, and as the taniwha slunk across the landscape of my imagination, Vicar began the worn-out rituals in a voice attempting to harmonize etiquette with empathy. *To lose a daughter as an act of faith.* Well. And he had seen her married, too.

The cries of the gulls whirling overhead brought home a memory of the escaping tide, sucking rocks and debris from the stony beach. *The sea*, I thought. Always with us, surrounding us, threatening to overtake us if we ventured out too far. Yet it was a risk I planned to take. The island with or without Ravenna could hold me no longer, and closing my eyes, I felt rather than heard the clods of mud hitting the coffin, interring my childhood along with Ravenna at the same convenient time.

The thin wail, louder than the gulls and more strident than the tide, startled me to attention.

Bent double in her fight with the grass and sandy soil, Auntie Faye let her hat slip crooked as she plunged, unseeing, into the middle of the flower-covered grave.

Timidly, Vicar backed away, and then became the head of a mass exodus as he waved his prayer book in the air, signaling the end of the funeral, and more frighteningly, the end of Auntie Faye.

Chapter Fifteen

Uncle Niall later described it as suspected catalepsy, but to the rest of us, Auntie Faye had just plain cracked. And in doing so, she formally relinquished all claims to protocol, leaving Auntie Pat and me to carry her stiff-legged back to the car she was to share with Uncle Niall.

"We will just have to ask all these people to leave," Auntie Pat said, as though testing the limits of her new authority. For the first time since I'd met her, her face had lost its bewildered flabbiness and she managed to regain, if only for the moment, what I imagined was her youthful vigor. "They can't possibly expect tea and cakes after this," she said before ordering Faye's driver to take her and Uncle Niall home as quickly as possible.

The driver of the car I took with Wendy insisted on following at a more leisurely and seemly pace, ignoring my request to let me get back to the city before dark. "I don't know why we have to creep home like this," I said under my breath as we inched through the exit gates.

Wendy jabbed the toe of her shoe into the thick, gray

carpet. "Appearances, of course," she said. "What else?"

But back at the house, appearances no longer seemed to matter. It was as if a cyclone had blown through, emptying our problems onto the lawn for the entire world to see. The front door, never left open, now stood ajar with Clare as a crumpled sort of prop to keep it that way. A few of the stragglers who could not be persuaded to go home converged on the drive, eating something horribly like wedding cake. As soon as we were parked, I fled the car to tell Auntie Pat I was catching the first bus into town, but when I approached the house, I saw her busy on the hall telephone and I had to wait.

"What's going on?" I asked Clare, expecting to be ignored. Blandly, she smiled up at me, then looked down the drive to watch Wendy carelessly trundle her wheelchair toward us.

"Mummy's trying to get Auntie Faye and Uncle Niall a flight to the South Island," she said, her jaw squared. Her tone made me look twice; gone were the sleepy twitches and the slurred, incoherent syllables. Overnight, while none of us were watching, Clare had improved, dramatically.

"Today? What for?"

"No one can face the local hospital."

Auntie Pat left the phone and loosened the scarf at her throat. "I've got Faye and Niall a flight leaving in four hours," she said. "That gives us time to pack their bags."

"Are you taking them to the airport?" Clare asked, letting her body go limp again when Wendy attempted to lift her into her chair.

"No, I've ordered a taxi." Auntie Pat gave her daughters a strange look. "Darling," she said to Clare, "sit up straight. It's not good for your spine to slouch like that." Auntie Pat straightened her own back and pushed her hair from her face with both hands.

"What an old pig's ear," she said. "Although in a funny way, I feel I've been expecting this day all my life." She turned when Uncle Niall came from the lounge. "Elizabeth and I will pack Faye's things," she assured him. "You go rest."

Uncle Niall didn't need to be convinced, and roped into a job I hadn't the time or inclination for, I went with Auntie Pat to the back of the house.

The heavy, closed air rich with talcum and the scent of ironed sheets made me hesitant to enter my aunt's bedroom. But Auntie Pat had no problem pulling open the mahogany dresser drawers and tossing toiletries into a bag.

"Here," she said handing me a pile of nighties and underclothes she told me to place on the bed by category. I did as she asked, and she added, "Why don't you stay with us tonight? Clare would enjoy the company. She and Wendy are always at loggerheads over one thing or another these days. 'Unfriendly' doesn't describe it."

Uncle Niall tapped on the door, arresting Auntie Pat's attention away from me. "Come in, Niall," she said, closing a suitcase. "It is your room."

Uncle Niall hung his head. "I just wanted some shaving

gear," he explained.

"Let me get it," Auntie Pat said, but Uncle Niall contrived a weak smile and shook his head.

"Save your energy for your own family, Pat. Clare looks pale to me."

"Clare's always pale," Auntie Pat replied, setting aside the items Auntie Faye would not need. When she was finished, she said to her brother-in-law, "Anything you want, just ring. Don't think you're imposing. Faye is my sister and I want to do my duty."

Uncle Niall secured his bureau and blinked his eyes several times, hard. I put Auntie Faye's extra slippers in her bottom drawer next to what looked like dried flowers from Ravenna's wedding. We were, I felt, in the midst of one of those domestic storms that either throws people together or scatters them apart. I suspected we were experiencing the latter and that we would never be whole again.

"Don't forget Faye's coat," Auntie Pat said. She gave the glossy buff mink a forlorn shake by the collar. "The weather in the south…."

Wendy stuck her head in through the door and said, "Taxi's here." She eyed the fur. "Shall I take that?"

"I'll do it," Uncle Niall said. Fatigue had brought new, unfamiliar lines to his face. He took the coat plus Auntie Faye's suitcase before turning to me with the closest thing to spontaneity since the gravesite. "Be here when we get back, won't you, Elizabeth?"

"Um—"

"She'll be here," Auntie Pat cut in for me.

With the taxi meter clicking away, further discussion was impossible. I followed Uncle Niall as far as the lounge to where Auntie Faye sat needlessly sedated on the couch. From her posture alone, I knew it would be a long time before I saw her again.

Uncle Niall helped her to stand, and then carted her off in a blur of concerned good wishes while Auntie Pat began to close up the house, collecting dirty plates and forks as she locked windows and plumped cushions. As she put the last of the cakes in the bin, she asked, "You are coming with us, aren't you?"

"All my things are at Rory's."

She frowned. "Rory again."

"You don't need to say Rory's bad for me." Auntie Pat tried to look like she wouldn't dream of saying such a thing, and I said, "I'm not going to stay at Rory's for much longer but I don't want to stay here, either. I'm going to ask Uncle Niall for my mother's money when he comes back." My words surprised me as much as they did Auntie Pat. It was the first time I had voiced a decision that must have been welling up inside of me for days.

"You can't mean it."

"I do. I want to go back to England. I want to go home and go to boarding school. It is, after all, what my mother wanted for me."

Auntie Pat seemed stricken by my news. She stared down the drive where Wendy was leaving Clare to wheel herself toward the garden, and said, "Don't think me selfish, but I have my own reasons for asking you to reconsider. Brian and I are taking Clare to the States at the end of the month. We're hoping it will distract her, give her a new interest in life. This paralysis nonsense has gone on long enough. There's nothing wrong with her and I'm tired of it."

I didn't know what to say. Auntie Pat had never let on that she knew Clare's illness arose from the same source we all drank from: an aversion to reality.

"We need you here," she concluded. "You have to help take care of Faye. Without Ravenna, she has no one."

"But I'm not Ravenna."

"You can still fill the void."

It wasn't the answer I wanted or expected, and clutching at excuses, I told her I would have to think about it. I raced to catch the bus before I had to hear any more.

I hoped Rory and Tania would be out when I arrived back, but Rory was on the porch, wearing a torn cabled jersey and studying a row of lighted candles. As soon as he caught sight of me, he ran down the steps.

"I know—I'm sorry—I should have been there," he said. "Was it terrible?"

"If you call riding in some kind of semi-hearse with Wendy and a wheelchair to a cemetery straight out of the Brothers Grimm, then, yes. It was terrible. It got even worse when Auntie Faye had a nervous breakdown."

"You're joking."

I sent him a look that had nothing to do with humor.

"I am sorry," he said. He pulled me back up under the cover of the porch and pushed a chair in my direction. I sat down and tried to breathe normally. The candles gave off a burnt-sugar, sooty smell that resurrected a time I couldn't quite place. My mother's flat, perhaps, after she and Lily had returned from one of their "salon days." Or maybe it was Ravenna's kitchen the afternoon she made coffee for her mother and me. Whatever it was, it made me feel sad and lost. I prayed the wind would blow the flames out.

"What happened to Auntie Faye?" Rory asked. "Did she start screaming at the grave or something?"

I dried my eyes with the back of my hand before I realized they were wet. "Close. She wouldn't let them finish burying Ravenna and then she went all stiff and just closed down. Uncle Niall has taken her to the South Island."

Rory whistled through his teeth.

"There's more. Auntie Pat and Clare are going to the States at the end of the month. She says it's for Clare to get better, but I think they just can't bear being with us any longer."

"I can't believe so much went on."

"Like you said, you should have been there."

"Well, you'll be free of them for a while."

I shrugged. "According to Auntie Pat, there's little chance of Auntie Faye recovering unless I go back to live with her again."

Rory's disgust was loud. "I hope you're not giving the

idea a minute of your time."

I leaned over the verandah railing. The sun was setting but I didn't feel like going inside yet. "No," I said. "But I can't live without money. The bookstore won't give me a second chance and I can't stay here. Not with you and Tania."

"Please," Rory said, joining me at the railing. "It's over between me and Tania. In fact, you could say it never began."

"That's beside the point," I said. "The truth is Tania was right when she said I was too young to stay at the flat."

Rory started to contradict, and I said, "Don't laugh, but I want to go to boarding school in England. I want to go some place where nobody can blame me for the past and then turn around to use it as an excuse to keep me from being myself in the present. This morning I realized how much time I've lost."

"Forget about this morning. I said I was sorry. But the thing is I couldn't stand going to one more farcical family gathering."

"You thought I could. Alone."

"You're strong, Elizabeth. You're probably the strongest one in this family. That's why everyone is asking you to stay, including me. There's something different about you that we don't have. You just haven't seen it for yourself yet."

Strong, I mused. Different. They weren't terms I would have used to describe myself, but if others had seen them, maybe they were true, ready to pull me through and help me become the person I needed to be. Not the indiscreet problem of poor Vida, or the unordered parcel that had arrived unwanted on Auntie Faye's doorstep, but me, just Elizabeth, just fine in her own right. The idea flickered through my mind that maybe this strength was a legacy from my unknown father. If I was strong, maybe it was because I wasn't really a Haddon.

"So what can I say that will make you change your mind?" Rory asked.

I thought for a minute. "What if you were to come with me? What's holding you here?" Becoming excited with my own plans, exercising my "strength," I continued recklessly, "Nothing you do here will ever be appreciated or recognized on the scale it should be. You have to aim for something more. Ravenna had so much, and she never used it. She just let things happen to her, like you did when you closed your exhibition. You let outside things get in your way. Don't you want to be in charge of your life?"

Stunned, Rory looked at me as though I had lost my mind. For a brief moment he appeared tempted by what I said, but then just as quickly, he retreated. "I couldn't," he said in a voice I had never heard him use before. "The idea is mad. How would I live in England?"

"Your art," I said feebly, but I knew he didn't believe me. Like Ravenna, he no longer believed in himself.

Rory blew out the candles, dripping wax onto the wooden floorboards. "This is my home," he said. "It's where my art—whatever that is—and I belong. Besides, I haven't told anyone, but I've had an offer. The school I went to in Hamilton is going to need an art teacher in a few years. I've accepted the position."

It was my turn to be stunned. And I finally understood the main difference between my family and myself. Their world depended on restrictions, self-imposed or otherwise, and despite my attempts to join them, mine was a place without boundaries.

"I feel I should thank you," I said, "because now I know what being a Haddon is all about. It's not 'carrying on,' it's cutting off your hands."

Rory averted his face, and as a tremendous burden of doubt and indecision fell from me, I said, "I have to be at Auntie Pat's tonight and I need my clothes. I won't be more than a few minutes."

"You're really going through with this?"

"I am." I walked down to my room where I collected my belongings, placing them in the same plastic bags I had arrived with only a few weeks ago. Undeterred, Rory came in to watch me.

"Are you coming back?" he asked as I debated whether to pack or wear the lumpy school blazer I had never managed to lose.

"To the country or to this house?"

"What's the difference?"

"I'm not sure." I could tell he wasn't listening, not properly, and I said, "I might be back one day, but on my own terms. I don't want to be like the rest of you, always looking at life in pieces. I want more than that. I want—"

Rory gave me a sad smile and dropped the hand he had started to lift to help me with my bags. "So it's good-bye, Elizabeth Haddon? If we can still call you a Haddon?" Before I could answer, I heard Tania call him from the other end of the house. He smiled again, and then ran toward her voice.

"Good-bye," I whispered into the emptiness. I returned to the porch and faced the sudden onslaught of wind from the sea. I braced my shoulders against its chill as I stood on the steps for one last time, letting the air rush and tear at me as the street lights came on, one by one. The sea air was cleansing and I hoped I could prove as strong as its determined current.

I could do it, I told myself. I would be in England by the spring and for once, nobody was going to get in the way, not even me.

About the Author

Valerie Storey lived in New Zealand for eight years. While there, she attended the University of Auckland where she obtained her bachelor's degree in Spanish. Valerie's favorite writers and influences from New Zealand include Katherine Mansfield, Janet Frame, and in particular the poet, James K. Baxter. Baxter's poetry is the inspiration behind *Better Than Perfect*.

Valerie currently lives in Albuquerque, New Mexico. She has also written under the name Valerie Keyworth. The author of eight books, she is now working on a collection of short stories as well as a new novel set partially in New Zealand. To learn more, please visit www.valeriestorey.com.